I'm

I'm Not Twenty Four...

I've Been Nineteen For Five Years

Sachin Garg

GRAPEVINE INDIA

Grapevine India Publishers Pvt. Ltd.
Plot no.4, First Floor
Pandav Nagar,
Opposite Shadipur Metro Station,
Patel Nagar,
New Delhi - 110008
India
grapevineindiapublishers@gmail.com
contact@grapevineindia.in

First published by Grapevine India Publishers in 2011

Copyright © Sachin Garg, 2010

Typeset and layout design: A & D. Co.

All rights reserved

For sale in India only

Printed and bounded in New Delhi

This book is sold subjected to the condition that it shall not, by way of trade or otherwise, be lent, resold, hired out, or otherwise circulated without the publisher's prior written consent in any form of binding or cover other than that in which it is published and without a similar condition including this condition being imposed on the subsequent purchaser and without limiting the rights under copyright reserved above, no part of this publication may be reproduced, stored in or introduced into a retrieval system, or transmitted in any form or by any means (electronic, mechanical, photocopying, recording or otherwise), without the prior written permission of both, the copyright owner and the above mentioned publishers of this book.

To all those people who live lives which are hard to believe.

Acknowledgements

To have a full list of people who have made this book possible, I will have to write another book titled People-who-made-I'm-not-24-possible. Here, however, I must provide the shortest possible list.

First of all, I would like to thank Durjoy Datta and Maanvi Ahuja, who continue to prove that MBA doesn't devoid you of your last traces of creativity.

Kshitij Bahadur, who keeps baffling me as to what the motivation behind those selfless hours of help to me, is.

Vipin Sharma, Shubham Joshi, Sidhharth Singh, Kanika Manchanda and Vivek Kunwar, roommates par excellence, for having smelt the dirty socks and armpits.

Aastha Jha, Aditya Gautam, Amit Arora, Avinash Chandran, Charanjeet Singh, Nikhil Joseph, Priyanka Aggarwal, Ridhima Khorana, Sagar Gupta, Sameer Kumar, Saurabh Vyas, Shruti Nishchal, Shweta Rabra, Siddharth Venkat, Sonam Sobti, Vedant Kanwar, Vivek Kumar to have graced the world's most happening corridor at MDI Gurgaon.

Ashish Sherawat, Garima Chaudhary, Mehak Gabba, Saloni Taneja, Seep Anand, Sunny Mittal, Surbhi Chugh and Vinit Gupta, for being living examples of the fact that a decade is not enough to get bored of me.

PGHR 08 and the MDI community, for giving me the confidence of taking the path less trodden, day after day.

Grapevine India family for their unwavering support and encouragement.

I also thank my nieces, Akshita and Rhea, Mom, Dad, Brother, Bhabhiji, Jijaji and Sister for their contribution to the events which has made everything possible.

Author's Note

A lot of people tell a lot of stories. But I believe there are basically two types of stories. The first type is when you read a story, and you stand up and say, *this is so like me.* You see yourself in the character, you get lost in their conversations and you fall in love with them.

And then, there is the second type, when you read a story which you could have never imagined and is from a world, you didn't know existed.

This is a story of the second type.

It is not even my story. It is Saumya's story. And there is one huge difference between Saumya and me. She is a girl and I am a guy. Now I really didn't know whether to tell this story as I was seeing it or in Saumya's own voice.

I chose the latter. That was the way to go about it: Saumya's story in her own voice.

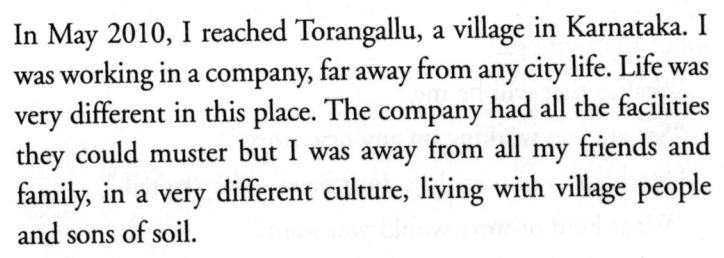

In May 2010, I reached Torangallu, a village in Karnataka. I was working in a company, far away from any city life. Life was very different in this place. The company had all the facilities they could muster but I was away from all my friends and family, in a very different culture, living with village people and sons of soil.

But the most intriguing part was that I got to see a very different world in that place. I saw incidences which I would have never believed actually happen. I had conversations which blew my mind. And I knew I was not alone. Anyone coming from a regular city will not believe this story.

I was going back to my home in Delhi when I met Saumya. I had taken a few days off for Diwali. The nearest airport to Toranagallu was Bangalore, which was 300km away. Saumya had always been quite famous throughout the company, even though I had never talked to her. There were not many good looking girls from Delhi in this company.

I saw her that day, and like every time, she looked very out of place. She had packed her bags for good. I could see that she was leaving Toranagallu. She was moving on.

We were sitting beside each other in the bus. It was a good eight hour journey and hence it was natural that we got talking. I knew she was from Delhi too, like I.

"You going home?" she asked.

"Yup. I am going home for Diwali."

"You are the writer, aren't you?" she asked. I had gotten a little famous in my company for my writings as well. Apparently, she knew me too from the company wide mailers about my writings.

"Yeah... that will be me."

"So, are you working on any new story?"

"Nothing as of now. Just don't have a story to tell."

"What kind of story would you want?"

"Real stories. The ones people would want to read."

"Oh. I thought I would tell you my story. It is real... but

then I am sure nobody will believe that it is real."

I looked at her. She was a regular Delhi girl, the kind I would least expect to see here. How had she landed here? And how had she reacted on seeing things she must have never imagined before coming here?

"I have a feeling you must have a very interesting story."

"I sure do. But the problem is… who even cares what is happening in Tornagallu? You should write a love story based in a college or something. That's what people want to read."

"You tell me *your* story and let me decide whether I can write it or not."

Saumya thought about it for a second. We had a long journey ahead of us. There was a Kannada movie being played in the bus. Both of us needed some distraction to shield our ears from it. Telling the story would have definitely been more fun than idly gazing at the landscape passing us.

"Okay. I will tell you the story."

"Great. If I do write it, I will make you the co-author," I said and smiled.

"NO! I am happy with my anonymity. You stay the author. It's you who is doing the tough part!"

I looked at Saumya. You would see her and would expect her to be wearing a skirt and a spaghetti top with a shiny face walking the corridors of a glossy mall in Delhi. But she was sitting in front of me, with her body tanned in places and wearing orange *salwar kameez*, with an unmistakeable smell of cigarette. And even now, she would make most guys stammer on speaking to her. It was just so difficult to get your eyes off her.

"But there should be something on the book which is yours."

"Not my name and not my face, for sure."

"Then tell me something you really love. I will put that on the cover of the book."

She thought for a second. And then something struck her. And a wide smile came on her face. She had thought of an idea and she definitely loved it.

"Give me your email ID. I will send you a picture. My boyfriend is a photographer."

"Okay. But what is it that you love so much."

"My shoes," she said and smiled. And then, she started telling her story, which I am writing here, in her voice, as she told me.

HOW TO GET TO TORANAGALLU

Toranagallu is in the heart of Northern Karnataka, in between Bangalore and Hyderabad, and almost equidistant from the two. It is famous because it is located in the hub of the steel industry in India and nearness to the tourist city, Hampi.

Toranagallu comprises of a small village of around 5000 people and some adjoining steel companies, where employees stay within company townships. The weather there remains pleasant throughout the year with showers starting from June till August.

Pleasant winds never stop blowing in Toranagallu.

All places mentioned in this book are real.

However, the names of some people and the companies have been changed.

PART 1: Babe In The Woods

Chapter 1
When I Get The First Shock of The Rest of My Life...

Hi. My name is Saumya Kapoor and I should tell you that I am a girl. Because Saumya is that kind of a name, you know? It can be both, a guy's or a girl's.

I have never really told a story. And this is my first go. So please excuse me if I sound really random.

Okay, so where do we start from? And how do we tell the story? I think we should start from how I landed in Toranagallu. That's where the story really began. It began that afternoon. Not so long ago...

⟿

It was two in the afternoon already. This was the only day in the two years of MBA, when all the nerds socialized with all the geeks and smiled incessantly for the first and the last time in their B school life.

It was the first day of placements.

The first day of placements at a business school is much

like a natural calamity. There is chaos everywhere. In a single day, tens of companies come on campus and fight for the best MBA grad in college.

On paper, I had no reason to be hopeful of an early placement. My resume was just better than ordinary. My marks were just above average and because everybody has an awesome list of extracurricular activities that they take part in, at a good B school, I was no different. Also I took pride in the fact that when you considered me on the whole, I had reasons to expect an early signing off from the placement process.

Lala Steel Ltd was a much sought after employer on the campus: Great salary, good brand and great exposure. They were known to hand over challenging work to new recruits as well.

When I saw my name in the shortlist for Lala Steel Ltd, I recalled that motivational video that I had seen on my laptop. I bucked myself up and lit up my third cigarette for the day. I knew that I was overdoing the cigarette part but I needed to maintain the energy level in my body and my voice. And it is always better to be energetic in a group discussion.

Group discussions can be hilarious.

"My friend, I would like to make the point..."

"Taking your point forward..."

"Friends, let's now analyse it from a merger and acquisition point of view."

The same sentences were repeated in every group discussion.

As usual, I cleared it, along with Amit this time.

Amit and I had been classmates in the Human Resource Management Programme at MDI, our business school.

"Congrats Amit, for the group discussion," I said, as I approached him.

"Thanks," Amit replied, without looking up from his books. He was that kind of a guy, one who never looked away from his books.

I didn't know him much. All I knew about him apart from his roll number was that his friends called him 'Humpty Dumpty' or just 'Dumpty' for short. I couldn't blame them. Amit did look like Humpty Dumpty. He was spherical in shape and wore specs. On party days, he would style his hair with kilolitres of oil. And worst of all, he wore his jeans high up, close to his navel.

Add to that his topper status in the class. That made him hateful by default.

Amit went first for the interview. The moment I saw him coming out of the interview room ten minutes later, I knew he was through. Amit was poor at concealing his emotions. When he walked into an interview being petrified under his skin, he looked it. This was the reason he was still unplaced at two o'clock in the afternoon despite his great marks. So today when he walked out of the interview room flashing the broadest smile on the campus, it was obvious that he had finally managed to not make a fool of himself in an interview.

Having seen Amit coming out with a smile, I took a cursory

glance through my resume. I had three minutes before the interview and I had to decide between another cigarette and washroom. I carried out a check on my energy level and realized that I could have done without stinking of cigarette. I opted for the washroom visit.

I looked at the mirror and saw my immaculately ironed shirt under the dark blue blazer. I saw my light black eyes and checked the *kohl*. The *kohl* gave my eyes the illusion of being beautiful.

Which they were not. I had ordinary eyes. But the good part was that I never had to apply any cosmetics on my face. My skin was naturally clean and fair enough. A gift which along with my good height (five feet six inches) and ordinary eyes made me turn my share of heads.

It's not that I am trying to flaunt or anything, but with all humility, my figure wasn't that bad either.

I came out of the washroom and said a short prayer...

With that I stepped into the interview room.

Two old-ish uncles were sitting in the room with a grimace on their faces. Their faces softened up on seeing me. Being HR heads of steel plants, they did not get to interview good looking young girls very often.

"Hi Saumya, Tell us something about yourself. And please don't tell us stuff already on your resume."

"Sir, my name is Saumya Kapoor. I am twenty four years

old and I am a person who believes in the simple joys of life. I believe that a smiling kid is much more beautiful than a Chanel bag and the sound of a river is much sweeter than Death Metal music."

Utter lie. The last time I had been between kids, I had wanted to slap them every time they smiled. And I believed that even death was a small price for Death Metal. But such descriptions are always a hit with old-ish uncles. A city girl who is not very shallow is their idea of Disneyland.

"It is great to see a young girl like you being so down to earth. How would you rate yourself on flexibility and independence?"

"Sir, I think the women today talk about being as independent as men. But when it comes to taking challenging roles, most of them would shy away. I am somebody who actually believes that women are at par with men and should rub shoulders with them. So I would love to prove myself by taking up any challenging role."

That was an even bigger lie. When I needed my cup of coffee I needed my cup of coffee; to hell with flexibility.

When I needed my shirt ironed, I NEEDED IT IRONED.

But independence, oh yes, I surely was independent.

"Are you sure you would be able to adapt to the challenging environment of the workplace?"

"Sir, I am somebody with minimalist needs. My father is an IAS officer. I have been trained in adapting to any new environment in no time because as a kid we kept shifting to new cities all the time. The challenge of coping with the academic rigour of MDI has trained me adequately. I have always been highly adaptive."

The IAS officer factor always works. My Dad is an IAS officer in New Delhi. He is supposed to have trained me to be adaptive. However, it only ended up in helping me pick the best nail polish brands from every city where we lived.

"Have you ever run away on being assigned a very difficult task?"

"No sir. I am famous on the campus for finishing everything that I start. I would love to take up any challenge that Lala Steel can throw at me."

My eyes shifted to my resume in his hand. Half the projects on my resume were actually unfinished projects. I had conveniently forgotten to mention the unfinished part there. I had this knack of finishing every project only up to the stage where I can mention it on my resume and then quit.

"You have any questions?"

"No sir."

I have always believed in replying a 'no sir' to that question. Asking questions shows doubt towards the recruiter. You might seem sharp, but no recruiter ever likes questions.

"Great then, All I can say is that I hope you would like working with Lala Steel. You will be joining on the third of May."

This was more explicit than usual for a campus placement interview. Normally they would say 'I hope you would like…' and stop. But this guy gave me my joining date as well.

I shook their hands with a broad smile and exited.

∽

Officially, the list came out at three o'clock. Amit and I both got through Lala Steel. So this was what everything had boiled down to. Two years of lying in the classroom. Pretending to sincerely believe in everything that I said in the presentations even though deep within, I knew everything was a hoax. My two years of pseudo-rigour reduced to me getting placed at Lala Steel.

Amit and I saw the list and we walked towards the mess where the whole batch was sitting. By three in the afternoon, half of them were already placed. The other half would be repenting one line or the other in their resume being still jobless.

Amit's shirt was torn apart in a matter of seconds. Vartika looked at me and motioned her hands pretending to threaten my shirt as well. But we both settled for a giggle.

"Don't worry we will do it but not here. Once we have reached our room."

∽

Vartika was my roommate at MDI. She played the role of that buddy who was genuinely interested in everything that happened in my life: Firstly, because she knew everything and secondly, because she always knew better than me of any situation. She even knew why nothing good ever happened to me.

Vartika got placed at a Cola giant. Hers could have been the worst resume in the history of that Cola. But she had the assets to make up for her shortcomings.

"So how are we celebrating?" I asked her.

"What a silly question is that?"

"You mean shopping, don't you?"

Vartika smiled. "This will be the last time we will be shopping with our parents' money," she said.

From the next day onwards, we kicked off our shopping binges. We set up insane budgets in front of ourselves.

I still had a month before my joining. I wanted to use this opportunity to finally do what I had always wanted to do but hadn't been able to do because of lack of idle time. I wanted to reduce the love handles at the side of my waist. My figure could have been immaculate, if only for these little lumps of flesh that hung on the sides of my tummy. They are the toughest to subtract from the body. I knew this would need a month of dedicated effort. But now that I would be wearing formals in the glossy Mumbai office of Lala Steel, it will all be worth the effort. It was really a small price to pay to be able to meet handsome guys in their formals.

I would walk a kilometre to reach the place where I could swim. I would start the day with swimming. And then I would walk back a kilometre to come back home. I would keep a strict check on my diet and would not let go any chance of walking. In the evening, I might go for a jog or badminton.

With that schedule, the results began to show soon. A simple brushing of the curve on my back revealed what I wanted to know. The needful had been done.

And as they say, when your body is perfect, people have no time to see your face.

Not that my face deserved being hid.

Suddenly, it was only a week left for my joining date. It was a little surprising to have received no information from Lala Steel at all after the interview. I still knew absolutely nothing about my job.

They hadn't even confirmed which city I would be posted in.

It was time for me to call up the HR and demand details. I had to be careful with my words because the lady could have easily turned out to be my future boss. The call could have become my first impression on my first boss.

"Hello ma'am? This is Saumya Kapoor from MDI, Gurgaon. I was wondering if I can have any details about my joining."

"Saumya from MDI? What? You are a girl? I thought you are a guy."

This was my name-curse, the sad part about being called Saumya. Saumya is a unisexual name. Half of India considers it a guy's name. While the other half thinks it is a girl's name, which it is, in my case.

I tried to smile, even though every part of me wanted to go

up to her and slap her right across her face. This is how the HR of the company made me feel special? By not even knowing my gender after having made my appointment letter and arranged for my joining.

I was hoping she was kidding. And also that if she was not, she might not have entered me as a guy in the official papers.

"Did you not receive a courier from our end? It was supposed to have been sent two weeks ago. It contains all the details including your salary structure and location and your train ticket. You should have got it long back. Let me check."

I heard some drawers being opened and papers being ruffled.

"Oh Saumya. It seems the courier was never sent to you. I am glad you called. I will get it sent today itself and you would get it by tomorrow."

The next afternoon, the courier guy rang our bell. There were only six days to go before I would start working. Lala Steel had its HR based in Delhi and Mumbai. I was unsure whether I would get Delhi or Mumbai as my job location. Every part of me was praying that I get Delhi. I have been born and brought up in Delhi. This is the city that I love to live in and eat out in.

Vartika had come over to my place to hang out that day. That's how we were killing our days until our jobs got us really busy. We just dropped by at each other's place and stalked people on Facebook together and made fun of each and every thing that ever happened on people's accounts.

"Still no word from Lala Steel?" Vartika asked, as she entered my house.

I shook my head and both of us made way to my room out of habit. We were both beginning to get a little tensed about the situation now.

"So you have Amit with you in the same company, don't you?" Vartika asked.

"Yup."

"Wow. Imagine if the two of you get into a romance. Won't that be the most perfect couple ever?"

"Shut up, Vartika."

"Let's stalk him on Facebook," Vartika suggested. I made a face. I didn't want to let anything related to Amit cross my mind.

Vartika started browsing his pictures and passing genuinely funny comments at them but I was too preoccupied waiting for the courier from Lala Steel to arrive.

My doorbell rang at two in the afternoon. Both of us rushed to the door to see who it was. Finally, it was the courier guy.

I opened the envelope and skipped the salary details. I always knew that I will get much more money that I can ever spend. I quickly looked for the train ticket and looked for the destination.

"Toranagallu!" Vartika read it out loud, shock reverberating in her voice.

I kept staring at the ticket in disbelief. Something was wrong. They could not have deliberately thrown me to a place with such a name.

"Look, in the gender column, the ticket says 'Male'," Vartika said.

"The idiots mistook me to be a guy because of my name."

It was the first shock of the rest of my life.

Vartika and I looked at each other, trying to understand what this meant.

"Let's check this place up on the internet," Vartika suggested.

Toranagallu is a village in Karnataka. The internet told me that Lala Steel had a steel plant there. The company has a township where the employees live and alongside, there is a huge steel plant. This is definitely where I was headed.

So this was it. This will be my first job. All my dreams of funky corporate life came crashing down in a matter of seconds. Steel plants were supposed to be men's world. Historically, only male candidates had been selected for such locations.

And then suddenly the implications of this information began to sink in. It must have struck Varitka and me together because she spoke it just as I thought of it.

"So this means that you have only two days left in the civilized world... The train is scheduled for the First of May."

I had to fulfil all my city desires in these two days plus pack my bags and leave for Toranagallu, god knows for how long.

The best case scenario was that I will be there for a year.

I, being somebody who needed her shopping malls and coffee shops within fifteen minutes of her home would now have to live in a village with a steel plant.

I, being somebody who needed her awesome plate of American Choupsuey delivered at her place within twenty minutes would now have to live in a remote village in South India.

I, having worked so hard to reach this B school, would now have to live without everything she always took for granted.

Life had taken a U turn in no time. Till now I had been so kicked about joining work. Suddenly, the situation seemed plain remorseful. Had I known the job location, I would have waited for another Fortune 500 company to pick me.

"What are you doing?" Vartika said, as I lit up a cigarette in my bedroom itself.

It took extreme situations to make me smoke in my bedroom in my house. This was definitely one, if ever there was one.

Life was a total mess. Take my love life for example. Being attractive and all, it was easy for guys to like me and they did. Whenever I would reach a city, I would find romance waiting for me. It was not the finding part which was the problem.

But this is India and things happen at their pace. The story doesn't end at establishing that I like the guy and that the guy likes me.

The whole process of getting talking, exchanging numbers, becoming friends, becoming friends of friends, becoming best friends, becoming more than friends, organizing a date, striking it off. And then kissing followed by proposing or proposing and then kissing was a whole year affair in this place.

The worst part was that by this time, my IAS officer dad would be transferred to another god forsaken city.

College was relatively more stable and a few romances happened. But they were nothing to write home about. Mobile phones had just become a household thing those days and the boy-friend-barrier in the country had fallen drastically.

In college days, there were troughs and there were highs but it was okay. I do not mind the troughs when I look back at my college days. What I mind is an absolute dead love life with no joy or sorrow. That was exactly what I had been thrown into.

All the tips I had collected over the years on office romance had been made futile by one communication gap in one company.

Chapter 2
My Last Visit To The Mall

"So what is the plan of action? What are you going to do for the next two days?" Vartika asked.

"I don't know. That's a tough question."

"I hope you have done all your shopping?"

"Well... err... I haven't actually."

"What are you saying, Saumya? Not done till now!"

"The fact that I had received no correspondence from the company until now had made me assume that my joining date had been delayed by a few months. So I kind of relaxed," I said.

"Oh! But it's okay. Two days should be enough for shopping for you."

"But actually, I have to meet my relatives as well before going," I said. Life had shifted from the first gear to the fifth gear all of a sudden.

Vartika kept her hands on her waist and made a face. "You *have* to shop for half a set of formal wear Saumya!" she said.

"Okay, okay! I will skip the relatives. Its only shopping, some friends and family," I conceded.

"But even then two days are too less," Vartika said.

My genius brain thought of an idea soon enough. There was only one way out of this hole.

I was going to spend my first day shopping with my friends.

I was going to spend the second day shopping with my family.

Purely ingenious.

The fact that I was spending my last two days in shopping marginally alleviated my pain of leaving Delhi. Vartika introduced me to a new mall in Saket and I must say that I loved the trouser collection that they had. I could go on and on about their collection and other shopping tips that each and every girl should keep in mind but this is not the platform. But still, flares are completely out of fashion. Please, please, please, for heaven's sake, stick to slim fits.

Vartika was desperate to cheer me up that evening. As we walked from store to store in the air conditioned mall, she kept raking her brain to find positive points about Toranagallu.

"See, everything in Toranagallu would be really cheap. So think of all the money you would save over a year. And then you can blow up all the money you get on shopping when you come to the city. Think of it as a lead up to the huge shopping festival you would have a year later. Won't that be great?"

"I am twenty four, Vartika. This is not the age to save! I want to spend all my money. Come on."

"Hmm... I know. Look at it this way. Because of the terrible food in that place, you can finally lose those love handles that you have on the side of your waste? Won't that be great?"

"Shut up, Vartika. Who will I show my hour glass figure to in Toranagallu? The buffaloes would hardly care. I so don't wanna go! And besides, I already have lost my love handles, bitch!"

Bitch is almost as versatile a word as fuck these days. Between Vartika and me, it mostly meant buddy or pal.

Vartika poked me at the side of my waist to check my absent love handles. I felt ticklish and laughed out loud.

"Well, I guess the only point is that spending a year in a place like Toranagallu will set your career to heights that cannot be scaled. Five years down the line, none of your batch mates would be able to reach where you are. You would be way ahead of them."

"This is it. It is time you stopped straining your puny brain. That Prachi has a job with Godrej and Venky got a job with Goldman Sachs. They will never be far behind. I am in deep shit."

"Yeah, I know," Vartika said, finally dejected. "I didn't want to say this but why don't you look for another job?"

"Well I want to, but those bastards have given me only two days to join. It's impossible to get another job in two days. I can't even let this job go because I could end up sitting at home. That would be intolerable. I am stuck, Vartika. Lala

Steel has cornered me from all sides."

She fell silent. She had run out of arguments. Even if she thought of something, I was sure I would have some counter argument ready.

She could see the spirits dropping in my stride. She had to suggest something to lift my spirits.

Just then, someone from the heavens above sent a Debenham store in front of our eyes. Debenham is the best brand in women undergarments available in India. We had walked past the display of this store thousands of time. Vartika did have a few items from Debenhams which she wore on special occasions when she met her boyfriend, Sunny. But I had not had a reason to wear funky lingerie since the time I could afford funky lingerie.

As we entered the exotic world of Debenhams, I found myself lost amongst the collection of well-crafted luxurious nightwear. There were dazzling camisoles, enthralling baby dolls and most glamorous bras and panties I had ever seen, with magnificent prints, chic floral prints and a stunning colour palette. The more I saw, the more startled, confused and desirous I was. After about an hour, we came out with a packet. The packet had a beautiful, cleavage enhancing black lace see-through balcony bra that started tight around the breasts, which then opened up in the middle and ended right under the buttocks.

Lucky are the women who get to actually use this stuff even once in their lives.

"But my mom would be packing my bags. She is going to find out," I said.

"Yeah I know. Chuck it, then. Anyways you won't get any chance to show your undies to anyone in Toranagallu. So what is the point?" Vartika mocked me.

While most people had been sympathetic about my ordeal, there had been enough nerds to pull my leg as well.

I hated it.

"I bet you a hundred bucks that I will definitely find some senior manager's son to make out with in that place. And he will be much hotter than any toy you get to play with in Delhi."

Vartika had taken offence. I was going to a village in Karnataka. I had told her that she won't make out with anybody hotter than a guy I will find in there.

"I will come with a bag to drop you at the railway station. You can tell your mom it is *aloo paranthas* for the journey. But it would have the Debenhams we buy today. I would love to know whether you get to open the packets in a year in Toranagallu or not."

"Sure. The bet is hundred rupees, Vartika."

She smiled confidently and I hated it even more.

Sunny was supposed to join us for dinner. He was Vartika's boyfriend. They had met back in their Engineering days and had fallen in love in spite of Sunny being a year younger than she. Their relationship had survived a few hiccups and they were now close to celebrating the seventh year of their romance.

Amongst a dozen qualities that Vartika had, I hated this one the most: the fact that she was so clear about her love life in contrast with mine – confused, dazzled and clueless.

Sunny hugged both of us. His curly hair had looked good. We moved to a restaurant for dinner. The whole dinner conversation revolved around only one topic.

Toranagallu.

"I have heard the Employee Mortality Rate at Toranagallu is quite high," Sunny said and chuckled wickedly. I wanted to break all his teeth in one clean punch.

"Won't it be great to be the highest tax payer in the whole of Toranagallu," said Vartika and both of them laughed out loud as if it was the funniest thing in the history of mankind.

"Make sure you stay away from Maruti vans with tinted glasses. Or one of them would stop beside you, open the door and kidnap you in no time."

Again, the wild and wicked laughter followed.

"Take a good look around this restaurant. This is your last time in a real restaurant."

"Statistics show that nobody has had sex in Toranagallu since 1997."

They both kept saying anything at all and laughing louder and louder. But they did not realize that I had secretly feared that everything that they said would come true. Behind my farcical smile was a deep hidden fear that life in that town might be unbearable. I wanted to cry out loud but grinned wider than before.

Chapter 3
When I Realize I Am Way Too Rich For Comfort

No matter how much I shop, my mom always manages to stuff everything I could have possibly needed into two bags. I had left the Debenhams lingerie at Vartika's place because it can be tricky explaining stylish lingerie to moms. Vartika was coming to the Railway Station with some *Aloo Paranthas* in a bag for the journey, if you know what I mean.

Amit and I met at the Railway Station. I had completely forgotten to ask his job location. He could have been headed anywhere from the Railway Station.

Amit came up to me and said "You know what they did? They threw me in some stupid city called Toranagallu. What did you get: Delhi or Mumbai?"

I smiled. I could see he shared similar frustrations as I did but I felt no sympathy. Amit belonged to places like Toranagallu. He was hardly using his Delhi stay in any way in the first place. I was sure he was secretly happy about saving all the money in Toranagallu.

"Well, even I got Toranagallu… Great, I will have company there."

The moment I realized what I had just said, I puked in my own mouth. I had just said I was happy to have Amit's company. I wondered if I had actually been glad to have him. I had pictured myself sitting alone in a room forever. Shit. Shit. Shit.

The sinking feeling completely took over. Mom, Dad and Vartika had come to drop me to the station. Vartika had brought the *aloo parantha* bag as promised.

The feeling got even worse when Vartika handed me over the bag. It symbolized what all I was leaving behind in this city. I waved good bye to mom and dad and turned around to see Amit. He was going to be my new best friend in that village. Imagine!

"What is there in this bag?" Amit asked seeing the bag Vartika had given me.

"Lingerie," I said. I knew he would not believe me when I would say that. And he didn't. He gave a confused expression and then fake laughed to save his face.

Amit did not have any annoying traits. But the sad part was that he did not have any pleasing traits either. You could spend a year with him and he would not say anything politically incorrect. But after a point you would want him to say something politically incorrect to kill the monotony. He could have been a good group person but having his sole company in a village was something I was not really excited about. His chivalry was going to be of some use, though.

Vaibhav Patil was waiting for us at the Railway Station. The train dropped us at Bellary, which was still an hour away from Toranagallu.

"That is some luggage," Vaibhav said, seeing the huge bags that I was carrying.

I passed a polite smile, concealing my irritation.

"Yesterday I had come to pick a family of three and they had lesser luggage," he joked and laughed with Amit. It struck me that moment. Amit had found a perfect match in Vaibhav Patil, both equally irritating.

I picked the huge bag containing my clothes and another one just carrying my shoes (formal peep toed shoes, formal closed toed shows, running shows, sneakers and my darling stilettos) and put them in the cab Vaibhav had brought to pick us. I had decided against bringing my Converse All Stars because lets accept it, everyone has a pair. Another bag contained my laptop while another had the knickknacks that I was sure I would never get in Toranagallu. To be fair to Toranagallu, most of this stuff was of the kind that you won't even get them anywhere outside Delhi or Mumbai.

"What is the smell?" Amit asked, as we exited the train station. The stink in the air struck us hard. I did not like how it seemed to be shaping.

Vaibhav smiled, in a You-don't-even-know-what's-going-to-hit-you kind of way.

The drive from Bellary to Toranagallu made all my worst

fears come true. If I had been living in the third world till now, this had to be the fourth world. The road knew no signs of concrete and the only traces of the developed world that I saw on my way was a Levi's showroom.

The bumps on the car had me dizzy and nauseous. By the time we reached, the constant motion had gotten me so nauseous that I was about to puke all over Vaibhav Patil.

Won't that serve him right for being the one to introduce me to this horrendous place?

I was woken up by the sound of 'wow' coming from Amit's mouth. I opened my eyes to see what had impressed him so much.

There was a huge board in front of me, with 'Lala Steel, Toranagallu' written on it. The world turned around there onwards. What struck me first was the immaculate gardening. Each tree was planted at the exact same gap measured by a scale. The colour green became the most dominant colour in the surroundings. The broken roads suddenly became so plain that you could ice skate on them. The air became so fresh that I wanted to go for a jog immediately. The depressing city gave way to the heavenly Township of Toranagallu.

The bus crossed the Sports Complex. From the elevation given by the bus, I could see that there was a basketball court, a swimming pool, a badminton court and a squash court. I thought I even saw the board of a PVR Cinemas but told myself that I had to be imagining things.

My salary structure had told me that I will be paying rupees one thousand nine hundred and eighty per month for my accommodation. They called my flat a 'quarter'. Coming from Delhi, the word quarter doesn't arise any happy feelings. The first image that comes to the mind is that of patchy distemper walls with shabby surroundings and a fan which overpowers the volume of the television.

Vartika had a heart attack when she heard how much I was paying for the room. It was impossible to imagine a room for which you are paying less than two thousand rupees to be liveable. But the moment I entered the quarter, I also had a heart attack, but in a good way. Being able to afford a two bed room, one hall and a kitchen flat in Delhi was a dream that ninety percent people die without fulfilling.

I turned around and looked at Vaibhav Patil. My look asked if I really deserved such a wonderful place to be living in.

"Well Saumya, welcome to Lala Steel."

I checked the washroom and I knew I would love to call this place home. This was Five Star stuff we were talking here. The first thing I did was call Vartika.

"Hey Vartika! One hour inside the doors of the Toranagallu Township and I love this place already," I said.

"What? Are you serious? I was expecting that you would be crying your heart out by this time. But how is the two thousand rupee house?"

"Dude, it's amazing here. If you visit me once, you won't want to go back. What's more, I have my own bath tub."

"Bath tub? Like the one they show in the movies? Haww! I always wanted to have one. But you know Delhi. I so want to visit you now!"

That felt good. I had feared that Vartika might reject these facilities and say that they are inconsequential in the middle of nowhere. She was highly capable of saying 'what use is a beautiful home when you cannot show it to anyone'. But she approved of the quarter. I even thought that she, in fact, was starting to believe that it might be fun to live in the middle of nowhere in a house with a bath tub.

I lit up a cigarette in my balcony and noticed people's curious looks at the cigarette in my hand. I took a shower and settled down in my room. The journey had been long and tiring but I wanted to settle down. Or maybe I just wanted to use the wooden finish cupboards. They were just too tempting.

I lined up my shoes in the shoe rack and took a picture of it and uploaded it on Facebook. Thirty seven people commented and forty two people 'Liked' it.

I used the hangers to arrange my recently acquired line of formal clothes. I had my own dressing table. So I arranged all my cosmetics on the dressing table. I liked the curtains in my room. I could see that some interior decorator had put in some effort to narrow down on the yellow curtains.

And then I dozed off. All the tiredness in my body ensured that I had a dreamless sound sleep.

I woke up relaxed. I liked the feeling. I had the urge to take a walk in the township and understand what all was available there. Moreover, on my way, I had made a list of things that I had wanted to buy as soon as I reached here. I needed toilet soap. I also needed a broom to clean my room. I put on my walking shoes with a pair of jeans and climbed down the stairs.

I checked my wallet and saw that Mommy had put in twenty thousand rupees for me.

The day was amazing. It was dinner time already. I decided to stop by at the restaurant they called the Converter. The fountains outside looked beautiful. You saw them and you felt like eating in that place.

Good ambience is the best appetizer any restaurant can keep.

I entered the lobby and my eyes were dazzled. That restaurant was at par with any you would find in Delhi. I was sure I was in for a big expenditure on the first day itself but I had decided to treat myself to alleviate the mood. Further.

The entrance mentioned something about their special North Indian Thali. I read about it and I knew that I had been spared looking at the menu. I was definitely ordering a North Indian thali. As I waited for the food, I went out for a cigarette.

I ordered Chicken Soup first. And then I ordered a *thali*. And then ice cream. The food was awesome.

I realized I had not seen the menu till now and hence had no idea about the expected bill. The waiter had been a little square till now. It seemed he believed I was another one of those city girls who would come here and pick holes in everything and then run away in a month, back to her pollution filled city ways.

When the bill finally came, I got a pleasant shock. In spite of the five thousand calorie delicious meal that I had just had, the bill totalled forty rupees. Forty rupees was like what you would have paid for it in the ninety eighties. In a restaurant like this and food like this, the food could easily cost a thousand rupees back in Delhi. This was almost curious. I wanted to know the story behind this. I called the waiter.

"Why is everything here so cheap?" I asked.

"Ma'am, do you not like it if it is cheap? People have problem if it is expensive and they have problem if it is cheap as well," he said in a mocking tone. I didn't like him and apparently he didn't like me either.

"Hmm… ok," I was in no mood to get into an argument. "But I don't have change. Here is a thousand rupee note."

For a second he thought if that meant I was tipping him the rest of the amount. But even in this serene city, the nine hundred and sixty rupee tip would be unprecedented.

"But ma'am, we definitely won't have that much change. This restaurant looks big but we don't earn that much. Please give me change."

"Well, I just told you I don't have change. It is your duty to arrange for it. Take this note and do something."

"No ma'am. You please call someone who can come here and give you forty rupees change."

"See I have just come here and I don't know anybody here. I cannot call anyone. You will have to do something."

"Just come here? What department will you be joining?"

"Well I have joined the HR Department as an Assistant Manager."

The waiter's demeanour took a U-turn at this point. The moment he heard my designation and department, he suddenly softened up so much that he could have slapped himself if I would have asked him to.

"Oh ma'am, you are the new Assistant Manager in the HR Department. Oh you are our guest Madam. Oh we welcome you to our small restaurant, Converter here. It is really great to see you Madam. It's is our pleasure to have you here. How did you like the food?"

"It was nice."

"I am sure it was. We take great pride in our North Indian *thali*. It's like our flagship item. Everyone here from the north loves it. And what were you asking? Oh why are things so cheap here? That is because the CEO has ensured that the employees don't feel any sort of discomfort in this beautiful township. So he has highly subsidized the prices of everything available here. It is very difficult to not fall in love with this place Madam. Moreover, we are here at Converter to serve you great food."

He was grinning so broad that I thought his teeth would pop out. The same man who had been a devil a few minutes back was now pretending to be an angel. I wanted to punch him and break all his teeth.

"Thank you very much," I said mockingly, trying to induce as much indifference as I could, in my voice.

"So Madam, let's go together and look for a change for a thousand rupee note. In Toranagallu it can be a challenging task to find change for a thousand rupees at a time."

I wondered what he meant by that. A thousand rupees was no longer a huge sum. I knew people who spent as much on coffee every week.

He took me to the departmental shop first. He introduced me first and then asked for the change.

"A Thousand rupees? Are you kidding me? It takes me a year to earn that much!" said the old shopkeeper and then he giggled like a school girl.

It was a strange joke. I didn't expect this place to have too many departmental stores. The only departmental store there, saying he didn't earn much was a little strange.

I remember I had to buy some stuff.

"Can I have a bottle of Dettol Handwash," I asked.

"Sure madam, it will be ten rupees."

The same Dettol Handwash would be twenty rupees in Delhi. The CEO had gone too far with the subsidization of all the goods. If I bought a bar of soap, a part of the money was paid by me and the rest of the money was paid by the company. They had an internal understanding. I could now understand why the shopkeeper's annual turnover was less than a thousand rupees.

The broom was seven rupees. I could have pinched myself to believe it. With dinner for forty rupees, toilet soap for rupees ten and broom for seven rupees, it was going to be a tough task to spend the twelve lakh salary that I was going to receive.

The waiter had been born and brought up in that environment. It was impossible for him to understand how shocked I actually was. He was just looking forward to his forty rupees.

How I wish they had a subsidized Gucci store here. If everything would cost half of its price in Delhi, half of Delhi's girls would love to work there for half the salary.

We then tried the vegetable shop and the milk dairy but to no avail. After that we came across an ATM, so I offered to withdraw some money and pay him. The waiter agreed.

I decided to withdraw hundred rupees, the least possible. I tipped the waiter with twenty rupees. After all, by the looks of things, I was going to be a regular at his restaurant.

Chapter 4
A bite of Iron Ore

My first morning at Lala Steel was a rather pleasant one. I was supposed to report at nine but I got up at six itself. I was so excited about seeing my office that I just could not go back to sleep. I decided to take a walk and check out the morning life of Toranagallu.

I freshened up and checked that the sun was about to come out, so I put on sunscreen on my face. I had some milk that I had bought the previous morning. I changed into my favourite track pants and T-shirt. (A part of me thought that the only reason I had wanted to go for a walk was to wear that T-shirt.) I tied my hair at the nape of my neck. I then picked my beloved sports shoes and was all set to go for a walk in less than thirty minutes.

The moment I left the guest house I was staying in, I became the centre of the universe. Everybody on the road turned around and stared at me. It was as if I was an alien in that land and everybody was looking as if I would eat them up. Being from Delhi, it's not that I had not been accustomed to letching. But the letching in Toranagallu was at a completely different level. I could see three people lining up at a small window to get a glance of me. I could see bikers going out of their way to check me out. It was plain disgusting. I could understand that this place didn't see too many women but this was outrageous. There was no way I was taking the road in this region in the day time ever again. And definitely not at night.

However, the township in itself was a beautiful place. Seeing it in the daylight, I saw the Sports Complex. Out of plain curiosity, I decided to step in and see the facilities available. The place had every facility imaginable to mankind.

The swimming pool was a beauty. But I knew I could never step into that pool. Being fully dressed, I was being made to feel naked on the road. If I was to come in a swim suit, people would be charging tickets to see me. Half the audience would jerk off at the sight.

The facilities available were top notch. The CEO had ensured that he provided every possible facility in this place. He had given us more than a few reasons to like the place.

⁂

By the time I came back, it was time for me to take a shower. I took off my walking shoes and went to the shower. After the shower, I finally got to wear my favourite formal shirt with my favourite formal trouser. The thought of wearing those clothes had had me very excited all through the journey from Delhi to Toranagallu. Being in them certainly felt good.

I then got into my three inch heeled stilettos. I couldn't wait to see heads turn each time I would walk in the corridor.

I had tested their sound before buying them and ensured that I buy the ones with the loudest clacking sound when I walk. I was sure that work will stop for ten seconds in whichever corridor I will cross.

Triumphant smile to self.

MBA had taught me the importance of using your physical attributes to your advantage. If you can advertise the fact that you are single then your attributes become doubly efficient. And if you are in a god forsaken place like Toranagallu, then they can take you places you can only dream of.

In case you are bold enough to spread the message that you are desperate, then the road to being a Vice President would be severely curtailed. Fortunately or unfortunately, I was far from being that bold. I wasn't even sure if I was going to advertise my singledom as that can always lead to unmanageable attention.

For the first day, Amit and I met in the parking of our guest house. We both had had our breakfast and exchanged a 'Hi'. And then we both looked at each other and the exact same question crossed the mind of both of us.

"How were we going to reach office on our first day?" I asked.

Neither of us had spotted any public transport till now. We weren't expecting to come across any at this stage. There was no way we could walk the four or five kilometres from the township to Human Resources office where we had to report, especially when I had my three inch stilettos on my feet.

We stopped a guy on the road and explained the situation

to him. Even though Amit was doing the talking, he kept staring at me. His assuring response confirmed that this was a common problem in this area.

"So, what you can do is just ask for a lift from any car which has space for two people. People here are really cooperative and the lift culture is really developed here. Just relax because you will figure out some way very soon."

He shook Amit's hand so that he could follow it with shaking my hand. It was disgustingly cheap. There was something wrong with the water of this place. Reaching office was going to be one of the many challenges of living here.

Once settled in the Honda City of an *uncleji*, Amit and I got to see the Steel Plant from up close. Everything there was huge. We were engrossed in appreciating the sheer enormity of everything in this place. The machines were huge. The spaces were open. The skyline was different.

I liked the openness of the space. Delhi had always been too cramped. The steel plant was as big as almost half of Delhi.

Uncleji entered a huge gate and in five minutes we got down in front of a building called HRD. Amit thanked *Uncleji* profusely for the lift.

We asked for Vaibhav Patil, the guy who had come to receive us at the Railway Station. He had been expecting us and welcomed us with a broad smile.

He guided us to an auditorium.

"Let's wait for Mr Malappa to arrive and then we can get started with the induction process."

"Mr Malappa is some senior person?" I asked. I thought it would be wise to know who he is when he comes.

"No no, he is another new joinee. He is just a Diploma Holder but has two years' experience with Tata Steel. He is considered an expert with Steel Technology because of his great knowledge. Once he is here, we can get started."

Amit and I nodded.

Ten minutes later, entered a dusky guy with a chewing gum in his mouth. He had a lean physique. Years of physical hardship on the Iron Melting Department had made his body extremely fit and fat free. He had an obviously goofy expression on his face. It seemed he had just walked into an amusement park to have fun. He was wearing a neat striped pink shirt with dark black trouser but his face just didn't go with his attire. From his expression it seemed he was still wearing a low rise jeans and a basketball T shirt.

"Are you guys the new joinees? This is the auditorium where I am supposed to be sitting, right?"

"Are you Malappa?" Amit asked.

"Yup. That's me," he said and took a seat alongside Amit. As he passed me by, I noticed he was wearing a highly elegant perfume. I had been wondering if I liked this guy or not. The moment the smell hit my nostrils, I instantly knew that I liked him.

He took his seat and introduced himself.

"Hi. I am Malappa. I am originally from Shimoga in Karnataka but I ran away from home at a young age itself. I have lived in several places but I did my Diploma in Machinery Maintenance from Jharkhand. From there I got employed by Tata Steel where I was employee of the year for both the years. I had to leave Tata Steel because my boss was insecure of my knowledge. He could see that in two years' time I would be his boss. He got me caught in a sex scandal and got me fired from Tata Steel. That's how I am here."

Ouch. He had a heavy Kannada accent in his English. The momentary bubble that he seemed to have created got burst that very moment. I can tolerate anything but an accent. He was beginning to seem cute until this moment.

Vaibhav Patil entered the room just when Malappa was done introducing himself. It had spared me the hard work of introducing myself and I liked it. I don't talk to people with accents.

Vaibhav kicked off the Induction process.

"I congratulate and welcome you all to Lala Steel Works at Toranagallu, India's biggest Steel Plant Location. As we sit here, some six thousand employees are working day and night to produce eight million tons of steel every year. I assure you that your career is in great hands."

He smiled as if to look for appreciation from us, which was quite absurd and totally stupid. How could he expect us to appreciate these alien numbers on the first day at work?

He continued, "The Induction process is a week long

program. For the first two days you guys would be visiting the various plants in this place. For the next two days, senior management people would be explaining to you the processes that you would have seen in the plants through presentations. On the last day, we would be taking you to the nearby tourist city called Hampi. This week is going to be a great learning experience for you guys. I would suggest that you make the maximum of this opportunity to learn as much as you can."

Unconsciously, my neck turned to Malappa and I saw his expression. He had stopped chewing his chewing gum and he was staring at Vaibhav Patil as if he had never heard anything more important in his life. His goofy demeanour had disappeared and I could see a potential Manager in him. Just as I was staring, he raised his arm to indicate that he wanted to say something.

"Sir, will the senior management actually spare time to explain the procedure to new joinees like us? It will be a great opportunity for youngsters like us."

Vaibhav Patil was elated at the remark. I would later get to know that Vaibhav Patil was handling the Training and Development Division at Lala Steel and he longed for days when his audience would be actually interested in what he was saying.

What followed was a five minute monologue where Vaibhav Patil poured his heart out on how the top management at Lala Steel was always very supportive to learning and development of youngsters.

The moment Vaibhav Patil left, Malappa immediately switched back to his goofy expression. He dug his hand in his pocket and took out another chewing gum.

"So you are really looking forward to meeting the senior management?" Amit asked him.

"Are you crazy? I can tell you already what they will say when they come to see us. Those guys have a practiced speech which they use to welcome every batch of new joinees. The moment I saw Vaibhav I knew that calling this guy sir and a little flattery would make him my bitch in no time."

I was impressed. This guy had taken his networking lessons. He knew when to behave and when to be himself. This accented guy was definitely sharp.

We were then told to move out where a bus was waiting to take us to the iron ore mine. We were going to visit a real mine. One hour ago, I had never thought that I will ever visit an iron mine.

A rickety bus took us to a mountain top which was supposed to be Lala Steel's biggest iron mine. It was a hill whose top was being blown off to dig out iron ores. But I was least interested in everything. The only thing I was worried about was how I was going to manage with my stilettos in those mines. The dust everywhere was sickening.

We were told to get off in the middle of a huge field where there was five kilogram of dust per meter cube. One could hardly breathe. The moment I stepped out, I knew my Gucci shoes were gone for a toss. The three inch heel which had excited me to death two hours ago now scared the shit out of me.

In half an hour's time, my feet hurt so much that I was almost in tears. They used to be black when I had reached. They were now light orange because of a thick layer of iron ore all over them. I took out a wet tissue from my bag and wiped my face in one clean stroke. I could have fainted at that moment. The tissue also turned bright orange confirming my biggest fears. My face now had a layer of iron dust all over.

I hated this place already. It had broken all records in terms of topping my hate list. I wanted to go back immediately to the comfort of my room in my house in Delhi.

As soon as I reached home, I kept my bag and went out looking for plain formal shoes. But finding shoes in this place was always going to be a challenge. I checked each and every shop in the shopping complex but could not find any shoe shop.

In the end, a guy in the shopping complex told me that there is a shoe shop in the other end of the township. I had to take another lift to reach that part.

The shoe shop was any city girl's nightmare come true. All they were selling were safety shoes which weighed a kilogram each. I had noticed that those shoes looked ugly even on people who were supposed to pull them off completely. I hated this place.

I decided to endure the pain of the stilettos for one more day but just thinking about it scared the shit out of me.

Tuesday was no better. Just that instead of the rough terrain of the iron mine; we had plain surfaces to walk on. On the second day itself, I had realized I was a complete misfit for this place in every imaginable respect. I so wanted to run away and go to a place where when people would like my figure, I would actually feel nice. Here, somehow it was plain disgusting.

Chapter 5
Who Will You Impress... And How?

Wednesday was going to be my third day. The plant visits were over. I got up in the morning and saw myself in the mirror. The only consolation for the sun tanning was that I had lost a few grams because of my incapability to eat the South Indian food. I was living on the North Indian *thali* at the same restaurant for every meal but I did not know for how much longer I could endure the same meal.

If you ordered a *dal*, it would have a flavour of South Indian *sambhar*. If you ordered Chinese, that would have flavour of South Indian *rasam*. You *had* to lose weight in this place. There was no way out. I was just waiting for the weekend to set up my own kitchen. And then I would learn cooking from YouTube.

Wednesday marked the end of those taxing plant visits. My feet had sore marks and shoe bites all over. My shoes had aged by a year in two days. I put in half an hour every day to clean my shoes after work. They got cleaned alright but they progressively aged by six months on each wash. So on third day, they looked a year old. What can spoil your mood more on an early Wednesday morning?

Amit, Malappa and I went and sat in the auditorium. Malappa was in his goofy college boy mode right now. So he went and clicked a few random icons on the desktop computer of the auditorium. He opened a presentation and mimicked Vaibhav Patil. He really was hilarious.

Once Vaibhav Patil entered, Malappa took the seriousness of a monk. No more fooling around.

Vaibhav Patil started the day with his usual nonsense. One could see that he harboured a secret desire to be a motivational speaker someday. But it was evident that he just did not have it in himself. Meanwhile, Malappa kept faking interest.

Then Vaibhav Patil started his HR ppt. The first slide he showed was on general rules of the organisation. It was the fifth point which made my heart sink.

"All employees of Lala Steel shall wear the company uniform on all working days."

My first two days at Lala Steel came back whirling in front of my eyes. Everybody had actually worn a light blue shirt with a navy blue trouser.

Oh my god.

This was catastrophic. I had spent my last two days in Delhi in shopping instead of meeting my grandparents. And now they expected me to wear that shitty shirt every day of the year. I suddenly had this urge to tell them, that very moment, how a girl can persevere in the most deprived of situations with her head held high. A fashion deprived existence although, is what scares us all. This is what keeps us going. This was what kept *me* going.

Waking up every morning to *idli sambhar* and then getting into the uniform like a commoner would be just way too depressing.

The relentless presentations continued from morning till the evening. Mornings now meant mourning. Evenings now meant harassment. We were being dumped with information that our brains were too slow to process. Retention of everything in our head was a distant dream.

On the afternoon of the fourth day we had the yellow dal and the orange dal, both of which tasted just the same. Once we were back in the auditorium, we saw that Vaibhav Patil was waiting for us.

"Hi, all of you. I hope you guys are enjoying this new world you have been exposed to," Vaibhav said with a glint in his eyes. That glint in the eye is an integral part of being in Training and Development. If you don't have that, people won't listen to you. It is the glint in the eyes which rivets people's attention.

Malappa was not going to let this chance go of networking. "Sir, have you seen the sheer magnitude of the operations in the steel plant? Oh my god! That machine just doesn't seem to end!" he said.

Vaibhav continued the glint in his eyes and told us how he had felt when he had seen it for the first time. I am sure had

Malappa pointed out something else, Vaibhav would have used the same lines in that context. These Training and Development guys can be summarized in one line:

All gas. No substance.

Vaibhav then turned to Malappa.

"Malappa, the next presentation is on Iron Melting Blast Furnace. The presentation will be given by Mr Manjunath. He is a General Manager at Lala Steel. You will finally be working under him. I am sure he will like you."

Malappa maintained a monk like smile on his face. I was looking forward to seeing this. It was clear by now that Malappa was a fun loving guy who knew how to impress his seniors. This was his ultimate test. I wanted to see how he impresses his boss.

Mr Manjunath was Tamil and he looked it. He welcomed us and spoke on his topic at which Amit and I yawned, pretending to listen.

Mr Manjunath clicked on the final slide and asked if we had any questions. Amit and I geared up for Malappa's onslaught of questions on Mr Manjunath.

Malappa didn't utter a word. This was possibly the first presentation after which Malappa had not asked even a single question. And this was his boss, the guy he wanted to impress the most.

Once Mr. Manjunath left we approached Malappa.

"What happened man? You didn't want to impress him?" Amit asked.

"Are you crazy? He is my boss. I am definitely going to act dumb in front of him. If he comes to know that I am sharp, then he would definitely load me with tons of work. That is something I definitely don't want."

"But he is the one who will sign your appraisal," Amit shrieked.

"*Arey!* Didn't you see the salary structure in this place. Worst rankings will get you only two thousand rupees less in a month. I would rather take two thousand rupees and relax my butt than work hard for two thousand rupees extra. Moreover, I can always work in the last month and impress him and get those two thousand rupees per month as well."

Amit was impressed. Here was a guy who had attended his Organizational Dynamics classes seriously and interpreted them in the right way. I felt disgusted. Making such guys work was going to be my biggest challenge in the company.

Chapter 6
Beer Versus Weed

The final day of the Induction week, Friday, was scheduled for a trip to Hampi. Now, Hampi is a temple city which is world famous for its ancient temples. Some people call it Karnataka's best tourist destination. I had read that the temples in Hampi possess mesmerizing beauty which attracts tourists from the world over.

There are two kinds of people in the world: Atheists and theists. I am an atheist.

But the best part about the day was that we could dress up in casuals. This was the only point that had made me wait for this Friday. I had obviously chosen my favourite pink T-shirt. I wore a pair of shorts because that is what you wear for a day out in Karnataka's weather. I will never forget the walk from my room to the bus in Toranagallu when eye balls popped out like table tennis balls on seeing me.

When I reached the bus, I realized Malappa was still not there.

"Where is Malappa?" I asked Amit.

"I have no clue," he replied.

"Why would he want to miss the visit to the Hampi temples?" I was disappointed. If Malappa was not coming, it meant I would be going with Amit and Vaibhav. There could not have been worse company.

"I don't know. I think we should get going. I don't think he will come now."

Ten minutes later, we left to see Vaibhav Patil in his office.

We reached Vaibhav Patil and he asked us to wait in waiting area. Ten minutes later, Malappa walked into the office.

"Hey! How did you manage to come? You even missed the bus," I asked him, trying to conceal the elation in my voice on seeing him.

"Haven't you seen the train tracks all over this place? There is this goods train which comes from the township to this place very close to Vaibhav's office. I got on that goods train and reached here."

"That explains the coal stains on your jeans." I grinned.

I looked at him and the coal stains on his jeans. This guy was rebellion personified. He seemed so aware of everything around him and so unflustered by it. I was definitely beginning to like him, in spite of his accent.

Vaibhav had booked a Tavera to take us to Hampi. He was supposed to come along with us but he got busy at the last minute. This meant the three of us were going: Malappa, Amit and I.

The drive to Hampi was a horrendous one. Once you exited the township and the plant, there is no sign of concrete roads. Had it not been for the shockers of the Tavera, we were travelling in, I might have had a broken back. Thankfully, we had left in the afternoon and it was going to be late afternoon by the time we would have reached. Otherwise the heat could have fried us alive.

Having spent a week with Malappa I could now see what the real Malappa was like. He did not have to pretend to be a good boy any more. He could be his chewing gum chewing self. In spite of his accent, he had completely managed to intrigue me.

An hour later, we reached Hampi. Our driver stopped in front of a huge temple. I had read on the internet that Hampi attracts a heavy bunch of foreigners. I had begun to expect to see some handsome foreigners but was disappointed. I wondered if it had all been a set of rumours, a marketing gimmick by the Karnataka government to make hapless Delhi girls look forward to exotic good looking men at Hampi. Or maybe it was just an off season. Either ways, the crowd at Hampi had been a disappointment till now.

But the temple itself was gorgeous. The temple looked mesmerising and yet so serene. Normally, beautiful temples in India can be human infested areas. I decided to give this one a visit for its pure architectural beauty.

Having covered the biggest temple in the area, we then

moved on for an evening meal. We hadn't had lunch and it was already evening now. I was starving. I was looking forward to having food in the restaurant called 'The Mango Tree'. Everybody recommended this restaurant at the first mention of Hampi. I was hoping to find some good food in this place.

The restaurant turned out to actually be a mango tree. A partial shed under that tree and a small table made the furniture of the restaurant. One had to sit on the floor in the ethnic Karnataka style to eat. The place had a serene feel to it.

I peeped into the others' plate to see how the food looked at this place. I was impressed. The three of us sat on the floor in a line. I made sure I sat in a corner because I was not looking forward to any conversation. I just wanted to savour my *thali* that I had ordered.

Just then I noticed that somebody had come and sat alongside. A very strong smell of weed hit my nostrils. I tilted my head just a little bit and noticed his feet with leather sandals and orange cotton pyjamas. He sat and kept a huge camera with a beak on the table. It seemed that a foreigner photographer hippie was sitting beside me.

I felt the curiosity to turn around and see his face and ask him where he is from. The weed smell was overpowering. I also had an urge to smoke up after the depressing week that I had had.

I turned around and all I saw were deep black eyes. He had a very sharp nose. It started from the nose bridge, where one would place his spectacles and continued in a straight line till the tip. He might have had clear skin at some point in time. But now, his skin was tanned at several places. I would have expected myself to see a sun burn at the back of his neck. His hair was dark black.

He looked familiar. And then it struck me. He looked so much like Hugh Grant, the Hollywood star, except for the black eyes in the place of blue and dusky skin in place of fair. One might say that that did not leave much. But honestly, if I would have taken a black & white photograph of him and tried to superimpose it on Hugh Grant's poster, I was sure that it would definitely fit point to point.

Strictly speaking, I had always claimed that I am the kind who likes dark skinned boys. But somehow, I would always end up crushing on the fair ones. But this one was dusky and it suited him. Here onwards, whenever someone will falsify my claim of liking dusky boys, I would know whom to point out.

He was wearing what one would call cotton Alladin pyjamas. The pyjamas were bright orange. They were so bright that one would have to wear sunglasses to look at them. On top of it he was wearing a white short *kurta* which exposed more than it hid. I could clearly see the outlines of his nipples through the translucent white *kurta*. I would have given him an age of twenty eight years which placed him four years older than me. Every detail of his that I noticed, I liked him more and more.

Just then I knocked at my own head. What was I doing? Seeing a guy and liking him for his looks? Wasn't I supposed to be way over that age? Was it just because of his nice face that I was so intrigued by this guy or was it the smell of weed? I reminded myself that I am twenty four and not nineteen. At twenty four you tend to lose the right to like a guy for a great face. You need to look beyond and find better reasons to like someone.

I convinced myself that there was more to this guy which intrigued me. Why did this good looking man look like a foreign hippie? What turn of events had ended in him sitting in Karnataka? Every inch of him seemed to have a story which I wanted to hear.

I wondered if he was actually from Peru or Brazil, from where people actually look like Indians in looks. But he looked more Indian than foreigner.

Sitting with Amit and Malappa, there was no way I could have struck a conversation with him. All I could do was hope that he does.

Meanwhile the North Indian Thali was served. It was heavenly. The *thali* had rajma, dal along with rice and roti. I fell in love with the *rajma* the moment I placed them on my tongue. I finished the dal first so that I could savour the *rajma* in the end.

As I was nearing the end of my meal, I was getting more and more desperate to strike a conversation with the guy. His orange cotton pyjama was constantly lying at the corner of my eye. I was desperately looking for a conversation starter.

"Do you like the food here?"

"Where are you from?"

"What brings you to Hampi?"

These were some possible conversation starters that I could have tried but decided against. All of them were too clichéd and too desperate.

Being a veteran with some thirty four crushes to boast of, I now knew that it is much more important for a guy to be intriguing than being handsome. Handsomeness can only get you noticed but if you really want to hold the attention of a woman, there has to be a certain level of intrigue in your personality. The girl has to find a certain level of mystery attached to you. Only then, can you sit beside her and make her desperate to talk to you.

And then a masterpiece idea struck me. I could have spilled my *rajma* and then the apologies would definitely lead to a conversation. But I loved the *rajma*. Would the sacrifice be worth it? Was I really so intrigued by this guy?

This could have been my last heavenly plate of *rajma* for the next six months. The decision was tough. I decided to leave the minimum possible that I had to and then spill the remaining *rajma*.

And I did. I swear I did. I was so proud of myself.

The *rajma* spilled all over the table. The guy stood up instantly from his seat. He was just in time to evade *rajma* falling on his orange pyjamas.

We were both standing face to face now. I could now have a full view of his face. Continuing with the previous trend, I liked him even more now.

I apologized fervently. "Oh I am really sorry. I spilled *rajma* all over your table. I am really sorry." I bit my lip listening to the lame rant that I had made.

"No, no. It's ok. My only regret is that you wasted a bowl of *rajma*. *Rajma* here is godliness. It's a pity that you deprived yourself of it by spilling it." He spoke in Hindi. He was Indian.

"I know! I loved the North Indian food during my stay in Delhi. I was missing the North Indian food like hell. I just love *rajma* but it's so tough to find North Indian food in this part of the country. It felt great to finally find it here."

I was now blabbering.

"I know. I just love this town of Hampi, especially this restaurant. I have been here for two months and I just cannot have enough of this place."

"You like this place? I mean I understand you like this restaurant but it seems there is just nothing else to do over here, isn't it? I mean there are things you begin to take for granted having lived in a city. But here you have nothing to do."

"Are you crazy? This is the most happening town I have ever been to. You just need to know where to look. I am not kidding. You guys need to know where to go and you will fall in love with the city as well."

He had now captured Malappa's attention as well.

Malappa joined the conversation. "So why don't you take us to some of these places. I would love to see what excites you so much about this place."

I could totally see Malappa getting along great with the guy. They both seemed compatible rebels.

The guy seemed elated to have caught our attention. "Sure. I would love to. My name is Shubhrodeep Shyamchaudhary. I am from Kolkata. I would love to show you around the real Hampi."

Malappa and Amit smiled in approval. I was looking forward to the prospect of spending some more time with Shubhro. Amit started to show some apprehension but Malappa ensured that we ignored it.

Shubhro led us outside the restaurant and then led us to some lesser taken roads of Hampi. We kept walking across some dingy roads of Hampi and I could see that the density of foreigners was progressively increasing as we went deeper into the city.

As we were walking, there came a point where the population reduced to only foreigners. We were walking along the bank of the river. There were no concrete buildings or houses as far as my eye could go. There were either shacks made of thatch or small huts made of tin.

He then led us to a small area where the river had reduced to a lake. The water from the Tunga Bhadra River had collected to form a lake. This pointed nosed Bengali had led us to the swimming pool of the foreigners.

I turned around to see Malappa and Amit. They were looking in a different direction and they definitely looked amused. They were looking at a bunch of white women who were lying on the rocks in their bikini. They definitely were eye candies.

The topless guys weren't bad either. There were men who cared the least about their bodies and ironically, that imparted them the most enviable physiques. The cigarettes deprived them of appetite and the whisky deprived them of carbohydrates. As a result, they become topless eye candies even though they won't be able to jog for five minutes.

Shubhro was smiling and looking at Malappa and Amit. He had been curious as to how they would react. He enjoyed their reaction.

We sat at that part of the river turned lake for some time. In that some time, four girls passed in their bikinis. A wide smile came on the face of all four of them on seeing Shubhro. They kissed him on his cheek. It was their style of greetings. Shubhro seemed one of them. Definitely, he didn't just know them. He lived with them.

He then told us to move on. He had other places to show us as well. It had now gotten dark. It was almost eight in the evening.

He then led us further into the city. There were no concrete roads in this area. Time and again, the smell of weed would hit my nostrils.

He took us to a big crossroad. On one of the corners was Sagar Bar. This is where he was taking us. He was taking us to a bar. Malappa was overjoyed when he got to know this. He had mentioned his true love for beer several times.

'Beauty lies in the eyes of the beer holder,' he muttered under his breath.

We entered the bar and one could have hardly told which country were we in. The place was swarmed with white men and women. The speakers were blaring old Hindi songs and they seemed to love it. It was a pleasant relief to have walked into a room and not be stared at.

Shubhro introduced us to the place. "This is Sagar Bar. You can get any drug you might have heard of, here. I stick to soft drugs though. Tell me, would you guys want to try something?"

I was surprised that I had to answer that question. There was no way I was trying a drug in this setting. Amit shook his head to say no.

"I might try half a light of weed. But I don't want to have the full thing. Would you want to share? Do you have rolling paper?" said Malappa. He had seemed the weed kind of guy from the beginning.

"Sure! I was looking forward to some. These guys will give you rolling paper as well."

I had never seen anybody high on weed. I wondered if he would look any different. I had no clue how the effect of the drug was different from that of beer.

The table and the chair had nothing special. One wondered what it was about this place that made it so popular.

Each one of the boys ordered a beer each while I settled for vodka with orange juice, the drink they also call Screw Driver.

Shubhro bumped into a French guy and the two of them kept talking in French for ten minutes. He knew French. Sexy.

Once he had left, Shubhro told us his name was Jean Cirillo.

One hour later, each one of us had taken in substantial amounts of alcohol.

I had downed three pegs of vodka.

Amit was two bottles of beer down.

Malappa and Shubhro were three bottles of beer and three joints of weed down.

Chapter 7
A Day Wasted

The mask of decency that we all had been wearing since we had met was now beginning to drop. The image we wanted to portray was being replaced by the person we actually were.

Meanwhile, the chaos at the Sagar Bar had also increased manifold . Shubhro indicated that he wanted to sit outside, clear of the bar's noise. He took us outside and we sat on the stairs. We did not have to shout to be able to talk any more.

I had a very strong urge to tell Amit that I sincerely believed that he was an idiot. I hated pretending to like what he said. I hated his heavy spectacles. I hated his round tummy. I hated his humpty dumpty kind of looks.

And I wanted to ask Malappa what he was made of.

Also, I wanted to ask Shubhro if he was single.

To make the matters worse, Amit wanted to tell a drunken joke.

"Once a black cat fell in mud. Then what did the white cat say to her?" Amit said.

I could totally see that I was about to hear the worst joke of my life. Amit was incapable of telling a good joke.

We all gave up after having thought for about a minute.

"The cat said Meowwwwww."

Oh my god. That really was the worst joke I had ever heard in my whole life. I wanted to get up and slap Amit. To make the matters worse, Shubhro and Malappa were laughing their lungs out as if they had never heard anything funnier.

To make the matter still worse, Amit wanted to tell another joke. "Achha tell me, if electricity wasn't invented, then how would we see television?"

None of us were in a condition to have thought of an answer. Amit eventually had to tell the answer.

"Arey, we will see it by the candle's light."

And once again Shubhro and Malappa burst out laughing. This was the best joke they had heard in their lives. But I had had it. Silence would have meant that Amit would have gone on for a few more jokes. I was going to tell him to shut up.

But I couldn't. All I could do was frown and keep sitting on the stairs and hope somebody notices that I was not enjoying the jokes. It was Malappa who eventually noticed.

Malappa was way too drunk. He had been blabbering for a while and was looking for topics to blabber on.

When he saw me upset, this was obviously going to be his next topic. "See Saumya, when a friend throws a joke, then you do not differentiate on the basis of the quality of joke. Even Gandhiji hated differentiation of any kind. When a joke is thrown, the person who is throwing the joke becomes the laugh-ee. And the guy who is listening to the joke becomes the laugher. The laugh-ee laugh-er relationship is highly critical in every joke. The laugh-ee might falter but the laugh-er can *not* falter, especially after beer. At least that was how it was in the boy's hostel. Don't know about the girl's hostel."

Amit stood up and gave Malappa a standing ovation for his speech. Shubhro clapped to express his appreciation. He looked unkemptly gorgeous in the dim light coming from the glowing board of Sagar Bar.

Amit said, "Very true, my friend. I cannot agree more. But who knows what happens in the girl's hostel. Girl's hostel has always been a huge mystery for us. We don't know anything that happens inside do we?"

They all looked at me because I was the one who was expected to know what happens in a girl's hostel.

"I am sorry to break your hearts friends but a girl's hostel is not as happening a place as people perceive it to be. It is quite overrated, to be honest. All girls do is gossip and discuss every possible thing about every possible guy and nothing else."

Malappa did not like my answer. He had heard different versions of some girl's hostel and he thought there was much more happening than I was telling.

"Why don't you tell me what you have heard?" I confronted him.

Malappa looked around and started his story.

"Well there are several stories I have heard. But my personal favourite is from my friend Saloni. She was pursuing her

Bachelors in English Honours from Lady Shri Ram College in Delhi. The daughter of the rich did not really approve of the college hostel and hence normally used to take PG rooms in the college's vicinity. Saloni had spent two years in the college hostel but shifted to a PG in the third year of her Bachelors. She was staying with two of her classmates from English Hons. The three of them were living in a single room and a single hall apartment in Nehru Place in Delhi.

A month had passed since they had been living together. Their comfort level had reached just enough to do something dirty.

The morning that I am talking about, the dirt was definitely in the air. Saloni had just taken a shower. There was a weird silence about the moment any one of them would take a shower and walk to her room in a towel. The air got heavy. Something seemed impending. It was simply avoidable by the simple act of taking your jeans or pyjamas to the bathroom. But it was a silent pact not to do so. Each one of them walked from the bathroom, through the hall to the bedroom in nothing but just the towel, once every day. The fact that there had been no males to the house till now helped.

Her two roommates had their necks craning to stare at her as she stepped out of the bathroom in her pink towel.

They had reached the point of no return. Everybody in that room knew that Saloni's towel would be kissing the ground in no time.

They all had gone silent as soon as Saloni stepped out of the bathroom. The safety point was ten steps from the bathroom.

She would have been safe after the eighth step as she could always rush the last two steps out of their reach. She counted each step and remained alert by concentrating on what she could see of them from the corner of her eyes as she tried to act as nonchalant as she could.

Five steps, no movement from them.

As Saloni lifted her foot for her sixth step, she realized they were not going to miss this chance. Both of them were all over her in a matter of seconds. Her towel was down on the floor."

All of us had the same reaction once Malappa was done telling the story.

"That's the best fictitious story I have heard in a long time," said Amit.

"You liar!" I cried.

"You were making up the story as you were telling it, weren't you?" asked Shubhro.

But there was no denying the fact that all three of us had loved listening to the nympho story.

Malappa finally gave his defence. "Okay, okay! I admit I was cooking the story as I was telling it. It was fictitious. But none of you spoke a word when I was telling the story. You all loved it didn't you? I bloody hell know that you did. Okay but now it's Saumya's turn. She would now have to tell us a story as to what actually happens inside a girls' hostel. All of us want to know. Shubhro must have never even seen MDI's girls' hostel. He deserves to know what happens inside a girls' hostel."

Malappa was very affirmative. He spoke with such conviction

that it was no mean task to turn him down. When he asked me to tell in such a way, I had to give him something. I could not have rejected the request outright.

"Well I can tell you what we guys did in one of the drunken parties. Don't get too excited because nothing of the sort that Malappa has told ever happened."

I took a breath and paused for effect.

"Girls' party are normally a very low key affair. Dressing up is mandatory for the party and booze flows easy and carefree.

My wildest booze party in a hostel involved just three girls, myself, my best friend Vartika and one more girl.

I wouldn't have told you guys but it's not like you are going to meet any of these girls ever."

And I grinned, suddenly feeling silly.

"So in this party, we three were pretty drunk and somebody mentioned a desire to play strip poker and the other two agreed. Well, let's accept it, strip poker has excited each one of us at one stage or the other. The rules were simple, that we play poker and whoever loses, takes off a piece of clothing. So the game started and the socks and the hair bands began to go off. And then came a stage when Vartika had to take her top off, first real piece of stripping. We talked her into doing it, convincing her that we will follow suit if we lose the next game. She took her top off and we hooted her. And what was worse, we ended the game there and then, before we were met by a similar fate."

The reaction to my true story was much more extravagant than Malappa's fictitious story. There was loud cheering. I looked at Amit and noticed that he was blown away. I realized that he was also from MDI and knew Vartika. Right now, he was busy imagining Vartika in the way I had described and possibly even fewer clothes.

Shit. The plan had gone a little wrong. But who cares after four drinks. He wouldn't even remember it the next morning.

Shubhro nodded. His pointed nose moved up and down. Delicious!

Shubhro had still not told any story. I had a feeling that he will not volunteer to tell anything. We would have to urge him on to start speaking or blabbering. He was a few beers and some weed down. I wanted him to speak. That would be a great excuse to stare at him if he would be speaking.

Amit was the first one to take the cue and urge him to talk.

Amit said, "So Shubhro, tell me what are your beliefs in life? What brings you here? Who are you? What is one thing that defines you?"

This was the best thing Amit had said since the day he was born.

Shubhro was taken aback by the bombardment of the drunken questions. He was silent but I could see that he was analysing if he could tell some things about himself. He was drunk and I was hoping he would be honest. It is said it is tougher to lie after beer.

"I might look like a common person on the surface but my life has been a story few will believe. Very early in my life, I had developed a very strong belief which has led to my life shaping up absolutely different from what it could have been."

He looked at each one of us to check if he had established anticipation he was trying. He had.

"I was all set to become a regular banker for Standard Chartered Bank after my MBA in Finance. I went to IIM Kolkata. But then one day I met a cousin of mine. He is six years elder to me. He was also a banker with Deutche Bank. I asked him about his six years of being a banker and what excited him about his job. When I heard his reply, I realized that whatever he said would never excite me. Once I would be in this job of being a banker, I might convince myself that it excites me but it won't.

The ultimate goal of my cousin was to become a General Manager of his branch office in Mumbai. From where he was standing, it was a great achievement. But from where I was seeing him, it was just so pointless.

I was asking myself some questions that have changed my life the way you see it now. What if he did become the General Manager? What was the point? What would it lead to? Is that all he wanted from life?

I didn't want the superficial materialistic excitement. I would rather look for a real excitement.

That night I kept thinking what I really wanted from life. On that particular night, I was sure I did not want to be a banker. I wasn't sure whether I would still feel this way the next morning. So I made sure that I mailed Standard Chartered Bank that I will not be joining them. This ensured that the next morning I will not have the option of developing cold feet and joining the bank."

The story had turned out to be much more interesting that I had expected it to be. Even his life had turned out to be more eventful than I had expected.

As he was speaking now, I could stare at him shamelessly. The more I looked at him, the more handsome he looked.

From the first moment on, I had been gripped by the mystery attached to him. Now, as he told his story, his mystery was unfolding. I was loving it.

Shubhro continued, "So I wondered what would really keep me happy in life. At that moment I developed what I called 'The Move On Theory' of my life. I decided I would keep moving on in my life. The period that I gave myself was three months. I decided I would spend three months in every set up and then I would look for a brand new ecosystem and spend three months there."

Shubhro paused to indicate he was done telling the story. I could see on Malappa's and Amit's face that they were as impressed as I was. We all talked about everything being pointless but how none of us had had the balls to actually quit everything and set off. Being born and brought up in Delhi, when a decent career meant spending a year in a forsaken place like Toranagallu, I did not even think of saying no.

Malappa had an expression as if he had just found God. I could understand why. He had always maintained that he believed everything is a hoax. Here was somebody who had proved that everything is a hoax and acted upon it. This was his aspirational life, the life he always wanted to live but hadn't.

"So where did you move to?" Malappa asked. The amazement in his eyes was still very evident.

"Well, I landed in Trinidad and Tobago with all my savings of my life in my bag. I was carrying a twenty kg bag pack and that bag pack was my 'everything'. My sleeping bag was my home. Life was on the move to the maximum.

I landed in Trinidad and Tobago and lived with a Jazz music family. Everybody in that family was in some way or the other a music person. Mr. Anderson was a saxophone player while Mrs. Anderson was a vocalist. Little Tina was learning to be a salsa dancer. I have never seen a happier family.

They smiled in good weather because it was good and in bad weather because it would help them appreciate the good weather.

I was having the time of my life. But I did not forget to keep on counting my days. I counted days until ninety and on the ninety first day, I left without even saying good bye to Mr. Anderson. I had to move on. This was the condition I had set for myself. I would have fun but would not stay in one place for more than three months no matter how much I like it."

Malappa's mouth was literally open. I am not exaggerating. It was as if somebody had just narrated his ultimate dream in life. I could not blame him. Shubhro has more to offer than good looks. Each one of us wanted to live his life.

"And then?" asked Malappa.

"Then, I entered Venezuela where I stayed with a butcher. His house used to stink so much that one could have fainted. But his daughter was gorgeous. I hadn't travelled as much to know this at that time but I now know that Venezuela has the best women in the world. When I think of Venezuela, I am reminded of two smells: one of rotten chicken that prevailed in his house and the other of Isabella, the butcher's daughter. We were pretty deep in love on my ninetieth day. But still, I left the place on the ninety first day."

Amit, Malappa and I were completely spell bound now, listening to Shubhro's story. The best part was that this exciting story was not even fiction. It was real.

"From Valenzuela I entered Columbia and then Peru. And then I entered Brazil. Oh god I love Brazil. I spent a year in Brazil. I spent the first three months with a family who were living on their earnings from the carnival in Sao Luis. You need to see that world to believe it. That was the best time of my life. God I love Brazil."

I could see that Brazil touched a different chord with Shubhro. He loved Brazil more than he loved the others.

"I then spent three months in Sao Paulo. It was great. Didn't I have the time of my life?

From Sao Paulo I left for Rio de Janeiro. I spent ninety days in Rio de Janeiro living in a dormitory. There were eight Brazilian boys in my dormitory. Each one of them was struggling to be a professional footballer. Each one of them was struggling to make ends meet.

We boys developed a bond that was quite unimaginable for me before I saw it. Those guys were living a tri-agenda life. Their days had only three things.

They would start the day with football practice. By the evening, they would have burnt more calories than a family of eight in Kolkata. They would then treat themselves with Beer and one prostitute each. I think Brazil is the only country where it is much cooler to fuck prostitutes compared to girlfriends. Girlfriends are headaches and boring. Prostitutes are convenient and equally beautiful.

By my ninety first morning, the bond between the nine of us had grown so strong that I could not leave. That was the only time that I let my personal desire win over my strong belief in the Move On Theory. But I am sure it will never happen again. Those were exceptional circumstances."

I wondered what had gotten him so excited. I thought I had an answer. With a bag packer as handsome and sharp as him, he must have slept around like crazy in Rio de Janeiro. The women must have loved an exotic commodity like him and thrown their panties and bras to his face. Nothing else could have given him so much fun. I was baselessly convinced that this was the real story.

"Like before, my families in these cities also woke up to find me gone on the ninety first day, without any farewell. Trust me, in those ninety days, I had thought of junking my 'Move-On Theory' many times. But I decided to stick to it except that once."

"But why?" Malappa asked. He definitely had a guy crush on Shubhro by now.

"It was the right thing to do. If I had succumbed in Venezuela and not moved on, I would have never got to see Brazil. Had I not left Brazil, I would have never reached Peru.

Life is not a sprint. It is a marathon.

Whenever I would have a doubt as to what I need to do in life, I would look at my life from a distance and I would get the answer that I need to move on. There is nothing to think about. I just have to go. If I falter, I know I would regret it. This is the deal I made with myself. As a result I have been moving on for last three years. I reach a place, I get used to it and then I leave it."

"Three years? Are you serious?"

"Yeah. In one month's time, I would have completed my three months in Hampi. This is the twelfth city that I am living in. From Brazil, I left for Lima in Peru where I lived with a Samba dancer. He spoke no Hindi, English, Bengali or French. He knew a little English and I knew a little Spanish and that's how we talked. I loved living with him. That's where I smoked the best cigars in the world. I also developed a deep interest in history staying there. I liked the way life was shaping. And then on the ninety first day..."

"I know. You left without even saying Good Bye."

"Yup. I did. I then went to Chile and then Argentina. During my travels, one question popped up again and again. Many people wanted to know that there when there is so much poverty in my own country, why I was travelling across these countries helping other country's people.

The only reason behind that was because I always believed it will be easier to help those people. I was less likely to lose focus and they would be more receptive to help. It was a baseless belief.

By now, I was beginning to go insane from the language gap.

It was time I succumbed to the urge of travelling back to this mysterious land called India. Everywhere I went, people were so keen on learning about this amazing country. I realized I hadn't spent enough time in my own place. I took a flight from Buenos Aires to New Delhi and spent the next three months in Paharganj in New Delhi.

I worked with a Hindi Theatre team in Paharganj. Their rehearsal place was right next to my hotel in Pahar Ganj. I heard the noise once and followed it. I found myself in a huge hall where Mr Ravi was rehearsing a play called 'Kal College Band Rahega'. I was instantly impressed with their acting skills. I knew I wanted to join them.

Mr Ravi agreed on auditioning me. I knew he could use an exotic face and accent like mine. The audience was bound to find me intriguing.

I like to believe that what clicked on stage for me was my I-do not-care attitude. The stakes were very low for me. If Mr Ravi would have liked me, I would have spent three months with his team or I would have found some other people. No big deal.

Once the nervousness was taken care of, acting became easy.

Mr Ravi added another character to the script of 'Kal College Band Rahega'. The play was to be staged in two months' time, which meant that I could stick to my resolution of moving on after three months.

Working with Mr Ravi's team was a great experience. It was truly a roller coaster ride. Besides, I wanted to explore Delhi from within and wanted to have insiders for company. The team provided me just that. Amit, Chetna, Rahul, Neha, they became my best buddies who would ensure that I see a new facet of the city on every evening when we weren't rehearsing."

I could see that Shubhro did not look back at those days too often. The conversation had shaped in a way that we were making him relive every day of his amazing three years. With every great memory, he started smoking a new joint of weed. He was completely wasted now. He could hardly sit and finally succumbed to the temptation of lying down on the stairs of Sagar Bar.

If only he was not this gorgeous, I would have told him that he looked like a beggar.

"I cried on my ninetieth night in Delhi. I had fallen in love with the city. I wanted to spend a life time there. Somebody please take me to Delhi."

Either Delhi struck a nostalgia that no other city had till now or the weed had taken over completely.

"From Delhi I left for Goa where I met a bunch of hippies. In the beginning, I thought that those guys were just like me. They were travelling aimlessly through cities making merry and sex wherever they went. Each woman that I slept with in the gang was great in bed. One cannot possibly be so gifted at fucking. Years of experimentation and repetition had made those women expert in every known detail of having sex. Those women were goddesses."

The weed had resulted in Shubhro's inhibitions being dropped. He was divulging the ugly details that he had been withholding till now. Many of his stories had hinted towards quality sex but after three weed joints, he was now explicitly describing his experiences.

"I got drunk as often as I could. My liver must have gotten rotten. Those hippies called themselves the uberos. Most of them came from central European countries like Hungary, Romania and Czech. I was sure at least some of those women must have worked in those awesome stripper clubs they have got there."

Shubhro's white kurta now had dirt all over. His bright orange pyjamas added ounces to his exoticness in the middle of Karnataka. I had developed a school girl crush on him. I was staring at him the way a school girl stares at a next door neighbour purely for his good looks and mystery.

"While I was in Goa, I had heard a lot about Hampi. It was only a night's journey from that place. So I decided to spend the next three months here. And today, I am done with two months of being in Hampi. In one month's time, I would leave this place as well, without saying bye to anybody."

Malappa's reaction to the weed was quite different though.

Where the weed made Shubhro talk and blabber, Malappa had now gone absolutely silent and serene. He got up from the stairs where we were sitting, and went and sat down at a distance, silently.

I could see that he was relishing every drag of weed entering his body. He was detached from absolutely everything around him.

Amit, on the other hand, had started missing some long lost friend after all the beer he had had. I wondered if this geeky thing could have some relationship history and if he was missing an old crush.

Either ways, Amit got up from the stairs of Sagar Bar, where we had been sitting and got glued to his phone.

That left just Shubhro and me sitting on those stairs. This was definitely a *woohoo* moment if ever there was one: Shubhro, high and out, with his undiverted attention towards me.

"So Saumya, you are done with your drink. You want another one? Let me call the waiter." Shubhro knew the waiter pretty well. One whistle and I saw the waiter was at my service.

Once the waiter was there, I placed my order.

"Hi. Can I have this cocktail called Screaming Orgasm?"

Shubhro laughed out loud when he heard this. And then he called the waiter close to him and said to the waiter, "You are one lucky fellow to giving this woman a screaming orgasm. How I wish I had the good fortune to give her a screaming orgasm."

At this point I broke down into laughter until the point my vodka came out of my nose.

Both of us exhausted our remaining energy in laughing out loud.

At the end of his fourth weed joint now, Shubhro could hardly speak. I looked at him and it felt great. I hadn't been this care-freely happy for a while now. It felt great to just let go.

Thankfully, at this moment, Amit hung up his phone and came back to the stairs.

Shubhro was in immediate need of a bed. But none of us could have had a clue where his bed was.

Amit had an idea. "Remember the French guy... what was his name... Jean, the one Shubhro had met in Sagar Bar. Let's find him out and ask him where he stays."

The idea made sense. Amit went inside and came back with Jean. The moment he saw Shubhro, he knew what must have happened. Amit tried to explain what had happened but Jean was least interested.

He slapped Shubhro twice to wake him up. He asked the three of us to leave.

So this was it. It was time to say an uncustomary bye to Mr Shubhro. I did not like the way it was ending. I had wanted to give him a hug. If the situation allowed I would have liked to tell him that he was really handsome and his pointed nose was the best I had ever seen.

But this was going to be the end. I decided to put a piece of paper in his pocket with my name and the Toranagallu address on it. Hampi was only thirty kilometres from Toranagallu. Maybe he could find time to drop by some day. I would have loved to see him again.

I put the paper in his pocket and we decided to leave. The alcohol was having its effect and the three of us bonded really well. Amit, Malappa and I we all three sang songs on our way back. The Hampi trip was a day well spent.

PART 2: Wood In The Babe

Chapter 8
Making the Head and Torso of It

I had the quietest weekend of my life that week. Saturday was spent getting rid of the hangover. All meals were had with Amit and Malappa, quietly. The company had ensured that the employees had every possible recreational facility within the township itself.

I spent the Sunday morning in the swimming pool. The way the people stared at me there, for a second I really thought if I had left my costume back in the changing room.

It was a quiet weekend. The noise and the chaos of the city already seemed distant.

On Sunday evening, we received our uniforms in our rooms. With a heavy heart, I folded each one of my formal shirt and kept them back in my luggage bag. It was depressing. It was like saying good bye to an old friend. It murdered the euphoria of starting a new life.

Monday morning, as I stood in the shower, the only thing that occupied my mind was that I was going to slip into that blue vertical striped uniform everyday beginning today.

I took off the towel and slipped into the shirt. I was horrified.

I needed to vent it out and I did what I always did whenever I felt like this. I called Vartika.

"Hello babes. How are you?" she asked in a jovial tone.

"I am not good, Vartika. I just got my uniform and it seems there is no difference between their uniform for guys and girls. Same cuts, same fitting, same colour. Can you believe that?

"As much as I am sad for you, I must say, I can definitely believe that," Vartika said.

"Was this why I starved every other day to have those shapely thighs and waist?"

This was seriously depressing stuff. Even venting out everything didn't lift my spirits.

We were supposed to start with serious work this morning. Which meant Amit and Malappa will be sitting in separate worlds as well. Neither of them was my best friend material but still they were human company nonetheless. Now I might be deprived of that as well.

Malappa, Amit and I went and sat in the auditorium like every day. We waited for our respective bosses to come and meet us and tell us our work profiles.

The first to come was Malappa's boss. We had already seen him as a part of our Induction process when he had come to give his presentation. The way he walked in, without a smile, I could totally foresee that Malappa and he will never get along.

I remember his boss's name was Mr Manjunath. He asked

Malappa to move to a corner of the auditorium so that he could brief him on his work. Malappa got up with a forced smile and went towards a corner.

I could overhear what Mr Manjunath was telling Malappa. "As the name suggests, Blast Furnace is a place where iron is melted so that it can be purified."

Malappa had taken offence. "Sir, I have already worked for two years. I would appreciate if you would skip the basics."

There. This was the first evidence of Malappa and his boss would not be getting along too well.

I was distracted by Vaibhav entering the auditorium. We had been told that our bosses would be coming to meet us. Did this mean that Vaibhav was going to supervise one of us? No!

Vaibhav stood in front of us with wicked smile and he looked at Amit. "Well Amit, it seems you have been put under me to work on Training and Development of the employees."

Vaibhav's wicked smile broadened and deepened. He was so looking forward to harassing Amit and making his life hell.

"Let's go to a meeting room and discuss your job role," Vaibhav said. Both of them left the auditorium to meet in a meeting room.

Malappa and Amit had now met their bosses and both had reasons to frown. Having a nice boss was a necessity if I wanted to survive in this place.

The next person who entered had an angelic smile on his face. He must be a man in his early forties. He had to be my boss.

Over years of thinking about my first job, I had mentally prepared a checklist of qualities I would like my boss to have. In the three seconds that I had between the moment he entered the auditorium and he spoke to me, my female brain carried a complete analysis of the checklist.

- Handsome? Well some might call him handsome in a Richard Gere kind of way. But my personal analysis would not have given him a very high score. He did have the oh-so-sexy salt and pepper hair but there was something missing. He would not make heads turn in a Delhi Mall.
- Amicable? When you start with your first job, you do not know anything. To make matters worse, you tend to have been living under the illusion that you know everything. In such a situation you need a boss who can hold his patience and explain to you everything with a smile. This guy scored a sixer on that front. As I said, the best adjective I could think for his smile was 'angelic'.
- Well dressed? I don't know how many people experience this but I cannot respect a person who is not well dressed. Unfortunately at Lala Steel everyone wore the same shirt, but still there are enough cues to be picked if you have the eye. This gentleman wore Hushpuppies shoes which got him a big thumbs up. His trouser was Blackberry. I wasn't sure if even I could pick a better combination in Delhi.
- Intelligent looking? Somehow you could say that this guy knew his job. I could totally expect him to extend an arm the next moment and utter the name of a premier B school as his alma mater.

- Spoken skills? One week in Toranagallu and I was beginning to get flexible on the language part. Everybody here had a different accent and I was trying to adapt to the same. I was beginning to convince myself that accents have nothing to do with intelligence or even sophistication.

Overall, I liked this guy. I could introduce him to my friends as my boss. He might just fulfil my secret childhood desire to become a crush struck Assistant to my boss.

He walked into the room and asked for Saumya in spite of me being the only one sitting.

"What? *You* are Saumya?" I had definitely seen surprise in his eyes. I wondered if it was the name curse again. He had expected Saumya to be a guy.

Did this mean he had carved out a man's job for me?

"Hi, I am Ashish Rao. I am a General Manager in the Safety Department here. I welcome you to the family. Let's take a conference room and let me explain to you your job."

His English wasn't like really fluent but it seemed decent. After all, he came from a generation before mine and this much leeway was quite acceptable.

We took a conference room. Until now I had completely missed the point that Mr Ashish was actually from Safety Department.

He maintained his angelic smile as he started the briefing. "Saumya, you would be working with the Safety Department. The Safety Department here basically has two responsibilities. One is to ensure that minimum number of accidents take place. We call it the 'Action Team'. The second is to take evasive action once an unfortunate incident does take place. We call it the 'Reaction Team'."

He paused so that I could assimilate what he had said.

"You, Saumya, would be working in the latter, as an integral part of 'The Reaction Team'. We have an extremely challenging and emotionally taxing job for you Saumya. Not everyone has the emotional capability to withstand the pressure that this job entitles. Your interviewer must have seen some exceptional ability in you to have entitled you with such a responsibility."

Exceptional ability, my foot! He had not even managed to highlight that I am a girl. And girls do not run around with accident met people. There was more gravity in the way Mr Ashish Rao was speaking than I had come to expect with people of his age. I could see that he meant it. I had seen senior people bestowing challenging responsibility before but this was different. There was a hint of grief in the way he was speaking.

"This job was earlier taken up by Mr Gunde Rao who had been doing this for twenty years. He was a hard man who could not be fazed by any circumstances. His sudden exit had thrown us off guard. You would be taking the mantle from him, Saumya."

There had been too much build up till now. What was coming next may better blow me away or my boss would have failed in impressing me in a big way.

"When an incident happens, the Safety Team has to take evasive action. One person has to take the victim from the plant to the hospital. Every second taken by the reaction team can have serious repercussions to someone's life. It will be the duty of you and your team to ensure that such a sin is not committed by the company. Once in the hospital, you will be handling the situation until the family arrives. There might be important decisions to be made. There might be tough situations which will show your true mettle."

He paused to see if I was internalising everything he was saying.

"Also, one of the most integral parts of handling the situation is informing the family of the incident in the right way. The usual recipients of the news are generally the wives or the mothers of the victim. So it only makes sense that a female breaks the news to them. You, Saumya, would now be that person at Lala Steel."

He was right when he had exaggerated the intensity of job to such a great extent. I was seriously blown away. He expected me to meet widows and tell them that they are widows and how it happened. For the rest of my life, I would be going to sleep haunted by scary voices of women crying their heart out and breaking the bangles on their wrists.

"I understand this is a tough job but I personally would be imparting you one week training for the same job and then you would be equipped with the skill set that is required for the job. Have a cup of tea Saumya and see me in my cabin at three o'clock in the afternoon."

He said that and left me to my thoughts. I had been daunted before by challenging tasks but this feeling was different. It was like I did not want to do this at all. I was trained to be mentally taxed but emotional taxation was not something I was prepared for.

I left the room. I heard Mr Ashish Rao pick up his phone and dial a number.

"Hey, Raman. You didn't tell me that Saumya is actually a girl. My uncle's son's name is also Saumya, so I assumed Saumya is a guy. The job profile I had designed was completely a man's job and I had a gentle Delhi girl sitting in front of me. But it was a relief to see that the girl is quite sharp. I have explained to her the job and it seems she should handle it. But you take care no such confusion happens in the future."

I had got the profile by mistake. It was all because of my unisexual name. I was plain dazed.

I spent the afternoon in a pensive mood setting my expectations from the life that was to unfold.

At lunch time, I heard Malappa and Amit crib about different aspects of their job but I could see that my problem was much bigger than theirs.

I was going to tell women that they were now widows.

I was going to tell daughters that they were now orphans.

I was going to tell mothers that their son had died.

The same afternoon, I went to Mr Ashish Rao's cabin in the Safety Department.

He had prepared a presentation to show me.

"How do you like horror movies, Saumya," Mr Ashish Rao asked.

I did not like the sound of it. This was a time which I had feared. It was as if my whole life had become a horror movie.

"Not much," I muttered and made a corresponding face.

"What I am going to show you Saumya is important for you. You need to understand what has happened before to avoid the same in future."

He clicked on his monitor to start his presentation.

The slide contained the image of a guy whose head had come in the Conveyor Belt. His head and the torso had been separated into two different parts.

A shriek escaped my mouth on seeing the image. It was the goriest thing imaginable to mankind. The image showed a real version. The head was lying at a convenient distance from the torso. The sight was sickening. One could have fainted at the very description.

I closed my eyes really tight as if light would manage to find a route inside my eyelids if they weren't so tight.

"Okay, okay. I'll stop this presentation here only. Let's discuss some theory on Safety in a plant location."

He said this and got into a presentation on the actions and reactions in safety. I heard him intently with all my attention. But the image he had shown me had scarred me for life. I would never forget that head or that torso even in my sleep.

Chapter 9
Babe Is Clueless

Mr Ashish continued with his presentations the next day too. He had told me about every possible situation that can turn out from a plant accident. Even though he had not shown any scary images, he described the scary scenes in as much detail as he could. I could draw unpleasant mental pictures of things I had never wanted to imagine.

Once he was done with the presentations, he told me to take care of Sridhar, a fourteen year old teen who had met with a minor accident on the road. He lived in a village just outside the plant area and had banged into one of the iron ore trucks of Lala Steel. I had to provide him first aid and ensure that he gets food in the mess. Basically, ensure he doesn't go to the police and leaves feeling good.

Sridhar was a true son of Karnataka. His Hindi was just adequate to be able to communicate with me.

"Hi Sridhar. I hope you are not in pain," I said and realized the stupidity of the question immediately.

"I am OK," he said. Like many people here, he was

uncomfortable talking to a girl. I wondered if that was why I was doing what I was doing.

"Hmm. Where do you stay?" I asked him to break the awkward silence. Talking would keep him distracted from the pain of the antiseptic as well.

"I stay in Toranagallu, the village part," he said.

"Hmm. What do you do? Study?"

"I do nothing. My family hardly has food. We are extremely poor. I steal leftover food from the plates in the mess in Toranagallu. I have been living on this food for a year now."

What? Living on leftover food? It was heart shaking stuff indeed. I compared this to my own cribbing about the dining tables not being wiped.

I wished I could do something for him but couldn't think of anything. I just wished him a get-well-soon and dropped him to his house in a company cab.

⇒

That evening I met Amit on my way back home.

"Hey, how is it going?" Amit said.

"Hmm, ok," I replied.

"Hey, what is wrong with you? You haven't spoken a word since Mr Ashish took you for the meeting yesterday. All is well I hope."

"Nothing is well Amit. I can't do this job. I was not made for this," I told him.

"You are always whining, Saumya. Cheer up. You haven't even started doing your job yet. I don't know what you do but I would strongly suggest that you give it a shot for at least a year and then you can switch," Amit said.

"One year? I am not giving it more than a week. I didn't study so much in life to be doing this."

I was clear in my mind that this was not the job for me.

Amit did not reply but I was convinced that he was convinced that I was being a misplaced babe in the woods.

I definitely was a babe in the wood. And now this was proving to be a piece of wood in this babe.

He sincerely believed that I had been given a regular job and was whining by habit.

Bullshit.

On the third day, Mr Ashish took me on a plant visit. He was going to show me the high risk areas where maximum accidents took place. I was so not looking forward to this. My life was getting progressively worse with each passing day.

I had been to the plant before. The first plant he took me to was an acid treatment plant.

As I entered, I saw huge containers with some strange words written on them.

"What are these?" I asked Mr Ashish.

"These are extremely dangerous acids being used in the plant."

"What do you mean extremely dangerous?"

"Well, if a drop would spill on your hand, it might burn it badly and leave a mark for life," Mr Ashish said plainly.

I looked at my hand and imagined a scar on it. And put it back in my pocket.

As we entered, the workers once again quit everything and started staring at me as if I was an alien. A week in Toranagallu had now helped me get used to it. I did not flinch on seeing this anymore. Some workers elbowed their neighbours to see me while others lifted their neck to stare at me. As word got around, some even left their jobs to come and see me. I was their latest show piece.

Mr Ashish told me of the possible situations that could go wrong in this plant. He asked me to come along and climb the stairs with him. He led the way and I followed him. The same plant looked quite different from the top.

One of the acid containers was being refilled. Its top cover had been taken off and three men were putting back the lid. It had a clear transparent liquid which looked as harmless as water. But the container had enough danger marks on it to indicate that it was extremely dangerous.

The marking on the container read hydrochloric acid, thirty five percent.

The three workers working on the container had not seen us till now. But as I asked a question to Mr Ashish Rao, my voice got them distracted and they turned their necks to see from where the female sound was coming. Once they turned their neck, there was no going back for the neck. They kept ogling and ogling. In their hands they had the levers to handle the cover of the container and their eyes were riveted on every curve of my body.

What I saw next was the most dreaded moment of my life.

As they had been staring for almost half a minute, one of the workers lost his balance. He stumbled in his place and he lost control of the lever in his hand. As a result he fell head first into the acid container.

The sound that he made, I am sure, will haunt me for several generations. For those few seconds, that he knew that he was heading into that acid. I could not even attempt to imagine what his heart must have gone through.

But he did not die immediately. The acid had given him serious burns but it takes time to kill a person. With whatever strength he had, he tried to climb the stairs inside the container. Once his head crossed the surface of the acid tank, his howling voice shook the air of the plant once again. He was successful in climbing three steps on the ladder. But then he lost his strength and fell back into the acid.

None of the onlookers could think of anything to do. They did not have the option of climbing down the stairs and giving him a hand. It would have proved too dangerous because the man could have pulled them down as well.

All they could do was watch and shudder.

I was literally shaking in my skin. The sound was penetrating deep into my body through my ears. In a way, I was responsible for what had happened to that man. It was my presence which had triggered the event.

"Somebody help him..." I shouted. But nobody moved. So I thought I would do it myself and tried to take a step towards the acid container but my legs were frozen. I just couldn't walk.

His screeching voice was falling continuously in my ears and I felt my skin falling apart. My heartbeat was fainting. I felt myself getting weak. It was as if an injection had been inserted in my veins and all the strength had been sucked out. I fell on my feet and lost my consciousness.

I woke up in the hospital. The first thing I checked was if there were any needles inserted in my body. There was a glucose drip entering my body in the left wrist.

The moment I got up, the sounds of that man's screeches came back to me. I wondered if I would ever be able to get over that sound. How will I shun all the thoughts of the incident that I had seen?

The best way to do that was going to block my head from stray thoughts. I saw Amit and Malappa and decided to indulge in as much conversation as I could. Conversation is the best way to keep the brain occupied and hence free from random thoughts.

The problem started when they left in the night. I was left alone, to myself. And all the sounds came back to me. If I wasn't lying down, I could have fainted yet again.

I wondered if I would ever be able to sleep again, as I lay in the hospital room, trying to sleep. But I was just turned restlessly.

I tried to ease my mind, but eventually called the nurse and told her I can't sleep. The nurse gave me a sedative and I finally went off to sleep.

The next morning I was discharged from the hospital. I reached my room and checked my mail. I had received a mail from Mr Ashish Rao.

Here is the mail:

Dear Saumya,

I must say the incident was extremely unfortunate and unprecedented. Even though we work in an unfortunate department and witness mishaps on everyday basis, what you saw was something even I have not been audience to in my seventeen years of career. I totally sympathize with you and can try to understand the shock you have experienced.

I suggest that you take a leave of as many days as you may deem fit and join back only after you have recovered fully on the emotional front. Once you are back, I would completely understand if you do not wish to continue working in the Safety Department. We can discuss a different profile for you and I assure you that this will in no way affect your position in the company.

Regards,

Ashish Rao

GM, Safety Department.

Honestly I was touched by the sweet mail. Mr Ashish Rao truly respected his employees and their wellbeing. But the mail had opened up a whole new question. Whether I wanted to keep on working on the same profile or shift to something less emotionally taxing.

I was too unstable to take a call. I knew that this was not the best time to take such a decision. I was sure that I did not want to discuss this with anyone. It was going to be my call. In the hospital, it was easier to keep the brain occupied with conversations. Amit or Malappa would stay at my pillow and conversation was easy. But back in my own room, I had only two options. I could either watch TV or watch something on my laptop. Broadly, both were the same.

I opted for the TV. The TV did not show most of the Hindi channels and Kannada was a distant dream for me.

I watched National Geographic Channel all day. I had decided I would make up my mind about the job on the next morning and as I saw the male panda licking the back of female panda, I had this urge to cuddle up with somebody as handsome as Shubhro. I wanted reassurance that life was not as horrifying as what I had seen. I was going to need a few days to get back to my bubbly self after the shock and I needed a manly shoulder to take me there. For the first time after reaching Toranagallu, I felt inadequate and incomplete.

I got bored by the time the male panda got bored of the female panda. I dozed off with the TV left on.

I woke up early next morning and went for a walk. There was no way I could think of anything except work. There were more than a few questions facing me at that moment.

Did I want to stay here at all?

Going back would have helped me erase the scarring memories faster. Finding another job could have proved easier but did I really want to quit so fast?

When do I get back to work?

How many days did I really want to sit at home and keep trying to not think of what had happened?

Did I want to be doing the work Mr Ashish Rao wanted to give me?

I thought of these points and I thought of my dad. Dad had risen through his ranks to become a Collector of his posting. He had seen more than a few missions in his young days. One of his favourite pastimes was to narrate gory stories to me. How would he feel if I told him I came back being scared of a sight that I saw? I ran away. I'm a quitter.

I looked around and breathed in fresh air. The horticulture contractor had done a great job in Toranagallu. The temperature at Toranagallu was always a pleasant twenty five degrees. The place always had a calm and serene feel to it. I was definitely becoming a Toranagalluyi, slowly but surely.

I don't know how but I had the answer that very moment. I had realized my answer to all the questions I had thought of.

I wanted to stay back.

I wanted to work in the same profile as I had been given by Mr Ashish Rao. If he believed I could do it, I would do it.

I was going to start work on the same day. I was going to take a shower after the walk and go to the office and see Mr Ashish Rao.

There was resolve in my stride. I had surprised myself with my surety and my decision.

Chapter 10
On Board and Bored

Mr Ashish Rao welcomed me with a smile. Actually, he was always smiling so I wasn't sure whether it was me or generally. But he definitely did react when I told him that I wanted the same work.

"Are you absolutely sure, Saumya?" he asked.

I nodded with a broader smile. I wanted to tell him that I am absolutely sure and that I am the daughter of an IAS officer.

He told me that he would continue with the presentations he had started taking me through. I was now beginning to understand what the challenges in safety were and what kind of Reactive Action needs were to be taken in case something went wrong.

He did not let me handle any cases that week. One of the employees had poured kerosene on himself and tried to commit suicide. He had sustained eighty percent burns but he told me to sit in his office and kill time as he left for the reactive action.

I logged into Facebook.

Vartika had left a wallpost:

"Not logged in on Facebook for two weeks? I think it's time I lodged a police complaint of you having been kidnapped."

I smiled but didn't have the creative energy to be able to think of a suitable reply.

Mr Ashish Rao did not let me handle any cases that week. We stuck strictly to theory. He wanted me to have recovered fully before I was emotionally challenged again. I got to know that even the employees were in a great shock after the acid incident.

However, the suicide case with kerosene was something quite regular. People were so accustomed to it that they would lift their heads to ask what had happened. Somebody would tell them eighty percent burns, could not make it to the hospital and they would get their head down again and get back to work.

Years of repeated incidents had made them immune to such news.

And all this was happening in spite of Lala Steel maintaining immaculate safety standards. The incidents were of the type where the company could have done nothing to avert them. The company cannot be held responsible for a man looking up to ogle at a woman while covering an acid tank. The company cannot be held responsible for a man committing suicide. Such truths were part of a Steel Plant with twenty thousand employees. The company had its constraints the way a human being has constraints. It was sad but then it was a fact.

The Lala Steel Township accommodated some fifty thousand people, including the families. In a town of fifty thousand, you would expect a few accidents here and there. But then, in a normal town, everybody doesn't know about every accident.

But in Lala Steel, everybody knows about every accident and that's what made it so scary.

I could understand that such facts must truly sadden the management but then even the management was helpless. Industrial accidents are as much a part of reality as industrial production.

I was now temporarily on sedatives. I could not have imagined going to sleep without that. So every evening, I would have dinner and pop in a sedative. And once my eyes would be too heavy to watch the TV anymore, only then I would go to bed.

After another amazingly boring weekend, I reported again on the Monday morning to Mr Ashish Rao. I mentally prepared myself for a tough day because it was going to be the day when I actually practice all the skills that I had been trained in by Mr Ashish Rao.

"Welcome Saumya, to your first real day at work. I would suggest you to stay in your seat. I will call you soon enough," said Mr Ashish.

I liked the fact that my cubicle was in one corner where nobody could see my desktop screen. Facebook here I come.

"Just go through these files and presentations of the previous year cases at Lala Steel. We have documented several cases and the reactive action that was taken. In case there will be an incident, I will be notified on my Walkie Talkie and we would have to reach the venue at the soonest possible."

I settled down in my seat and opened the first presentation. By the time I reached the seventeenth slide, I was terribly sleepy. There onwards I was reading only with my eyes. By the thirty second slide, even my eyes started betraying me and began to droop like mango laden branches.

Suddenly, in the middle of the afternoon, I realized it was lunch hour. Some alert part of my brain had been signalling my index finger to change the slide of the presentation but my brain registered absolutely nothing.

I had lunch alone which was as depressing as I had expected it to be.

Post lunch, the same thing followed. Mr Ashish had given me enough presentations to last a month. It was time I clicked on www.facebook.com. The moment I clicked on Facebook, every trace of my sleep was gone.

No incidents were reported on that day or on the next day. Suddenly, I transformed from being absent from Facebook to being Facebook crazy. I left comments on every photograph posted in last one month and played games I had always believed to be too stupid.

It was on the fourth day that I got my first call. One of the employees had got a heart attack at work. He worked in the pellet plant.

I had been to the pellet plant. All I remembered was iron dust all over. One could hardly see beyond fifteen meters in that plant. It was a very depressing place to work at.

Mr Ashish and I got into his jeep and headed for the pellet plant. By the time we reached, the patient was being put into an Ambulance. Seeing the patient gave me the shock of my life.

The guy was a young man who could not have been any more than twenty five years. A heart attack at this age was unthinkable. Mr Ashish talked to the shift in charge of the pellet plant and told me that he and I were the only ones going to the Hospital.

By the time we reached the Hospital, the patient was already in the Operation Theatre. The doctors did not wait for any paper work or any signature. They were accustomed to handling Lala Steel employees and they knew that best treatment had to be their top priority. Everything would definitely be taken care of.

The operation lasted eight hours. My heart was pounding. My brain had been drawing the possibilities all this time in the waiting room. Mr Ashish on the other hand seemed more at ease. He had read the whole newspaper and every magazine in the waiting room. I couldn't help imagining how he would react to whatever news the doctors might bring. Was he really immune to such news?

When the doctors came out, the answer was written all over

their face. The name plate of his office had told me his name was Dr Om Prakash Sharma.

"He is safe. You can inform his family, he is alright," Dr Om Prakash said and left.

This was where my real job began. Explaining the whole situation to his family and ensuring that they understood things were now under control.

Mr. Ashish looked at me and showed me his mobile screen. It had the patient's mother's contact details.

"But I need more information before I talk to her. There is more to the incident that I don't know. How can I talk to her before I talk to the doctor? I don't even know what had happened to this guy."

Mr Ashish understood what I meant. He told me to go to the doctor's cabin and see him.

The doctor seemed a little surprised on seeing me. It seemed to me that my predecessor had never been interested in collecting any sort of information.

But still, the doctor seemed cooperative enough to provide all the information.

"Madam, this young man just experienced a severe heart stroke. He must be approximately twenty four years of age and heart attacks at such ages are a rare incident. But he has only himself to blame. I can see that he works in a place where there is a lot of iron dust. This guy seems to never wash his mouth or hands after work. As a result, over the years, the iron dust has gotten accumulated in his veins and stomach. Such iron dust was beginning to cause his blood pressure to rise.

Today, the situation got out of hand and it caused a heart attack."

Ouch. It was a really sad story to break to a mother. I had my work cut out. I now knew why my job was considered such a tough one. I groped my head for all the theory that Mr Ashish had loaded on me in one week. Nothing seemed even remotely relevant.

I was about to make the most difficult phone call of my life. I was to tell a mother/ sister that her son/ brother had just escaped death. She would take forty hours to reach Toranagallu. She would live hell for the next forty hours. That too, if she can afford the train ticket and also manage to get her hands on the ticket.

"Hello?" I finally made the call without having a hint or a clue as to what I was going to say.

"Hello?" It sounded like his mother. Shit. I was hoping it will be his sister. Sisters are a little more rational. You can explain to them what has happened but things are under control. Mothers are more likely to break down at the very mention of the words 'heart attack'.

"Hello ma'am. Mai Saumya bol rahi hu Lala Steel se."

Obviously I had to stick to Hindi. Such news cannot be discussed in English with mothers.

"Haa Saumya beti. Bolo. Sab theek toh hai na?" Aunty asked. She sounded quite hassled already. This was not a good sign. If the fact that Lala Steel was calling her up could disconcert her so much, I wondered how hard the actual news will hit.

"Yes Aunty. Now everything is alright. Rohan had gotten

unwell this morning but now he is absolutely OK."

Start with telling that things are under control, one of the presentations had said. Establishing the fact that things are back to normal before proceeding is important.

"Why? What happened to Rohan? Did he fall off the bike?" She was shrieking. It was pandemonium in her life. My worst fears had come true. She was panicking.

It was evident that her heart was palpating. I could feel the anguish of a mother. I could feel deep inside my chest. It was time for the tough part. It was time to tell her that it was a heart attack.

"Aunty use ek minor heart attack aya tha. Par ab woh bilkul theek hai. Doctors ne kaha woh agle hafte se kaam pe bhi ja sakta hai."

("Aunty he had had a mild heart attack but he is absolutely alright now. Doctors said he can get back to work from next week.")

"Heart attack…?" was all she could muster. Words failed her completely. I heard sounds from the back of people noticing that she was on the phone and just received some terrible news.

I heard some sounds from the back. A male voice shouted '*kya hua?*' in panic at Rohan's mother.

It must have been Rohan's father who picked the phone next. He was in equal panic.

I explained the whole situation to him.

"I always knew that it's not a good idea to work in a steel plant. Give the phone to him. I am coming to pick him up today itself." As compared to Rohan's mother, Rohan's father seemed to be angry rather than panicking, as if it was the company's fault that Rohan was here.

"Uncle he is still not conscious. But he will soon gain consciousness."

"Toh beta doctor se hi baat kara do."

"Jee achha, Uncle."

I found the doctor and gave the phone to him.

And sat down to decipher what exactly had happened.

This was the end of my first assignment. Informing the family was done. Now all I had to do was to ensure that Rohan talks to his mother when he gains consciousness. The panic in his mother's voice had struck something deep inside my body. I was shaken to the core.

The fact that a woman was breaking the news helped the cause a lot. Had the same news been delivered by Mr Ashish, Rohan's mother would have straight away started abusing the company. Mr. Ashish being the voice of the company would have faced the brunt as if he was the man responsible for everything.

'Challenging' was a gross understatement for my job.

Chapter 11
That Stare Which Pierces Through Everything

The next day, Mr Ashish got back to his cabin in the Safety Department. I was supposed to stay with Rohan until he was absolutely stable again. That was going to take another day, the doctors had told me. The next day I was back in my cubicle. The voice of Rohan's mother was still resonating in my head. I was still quite disturbed. I was once again clouded by doubts; whether I was capable of handling this pressure and this environment. And once again, I fooled myself into believing that I was overestimating the difficulty level.

I went to the washroom and looked at myself. My eyes had developed dark circles under them. I couldn't sleep a blink without a sedative. Even when I was sitting alone, I would have flashes of sights picked from the scariest of horror movies. My hair had lost its shine. Hair fall had been higher than ever before.

In short, I was a mess.

The pre-lunch half went okay. I used Facebook to stay distracted. My only focus these days was to stay distracted. A few of Vartika's posts actually made me break into a loud laugh which I had to check to maintain the office decorum.

The next ten days were mostly eventless. I downloaded a few e-books and read them one after the other. Once they were over, I shifted to reading blogs. Blogs were much more comfortable to read. My hobbies were shifting from what a regular twenty four year old would like to more boring activities. I had heard stories of office boredom. Now I could relate to all the stories. Spending three days pretending to be busy was tough. For a tiny second, I wondered if actually getting a case would be better than this torture. The answer was a resounding *NO*.

On the eleventh day, we finally got a call. The call was from the Mill section. Apparently, a man's right arm had gotten stuck in a Conveyor Belt.

Mr Ashish Rao rushed to his car. I mentally prepared myself for what I was going to see. Being mentally prepared should cushion the shock when I see it. I told myself that it cannot be worse than what I had already seen.

I might have been wrong. The man's hand had undergone a complete cut and fallen off. The sight was no less scary than what I had seen. The rest of his hand was still stuck in the conveyor belt and the man was writhing in serious pain. He was howling from time to time. Some mechanics were trying to disintegrate the machine so that his hand could come out. An ambulance was standing there, waiting for him to get free so that he could be taken to the hospital.

If his hand was not freed fast enough, excessive bleeding

could cost him his life. The mechanics were in a state of panic as they shuttled tool after tool to break open the conveyor belt. The victim was fast beginning to lose consciousness.

Seeing Mr Ashish Rao, one of the labourers came up voluntarily and started narrating the story without being asked to.

"Sir, this guy was cleaning the belt in this area. The belt was stopped for a while for maintenance. His supervisor told him to finish off the task as the maintenance was going on. Once the maintenance was done, the rest of the people forgot to check whether he was done with the work or not. Somebody turned on the conveyor belt and the next thing we knew was that he was stuck here like this."

Industrial accidents make a sad story each and every time. And you can blame each and every one of them to pure bad luck. Contrary to my expectations, even though this was effectively my third case, the sight of blood and the sound of a man writhing in pain made me really weak.

I was completely capable of fainting had I let go of myself. My body did take the first step towards fainting but I told myself to withstand the weakness. One had to be there to understand it. It was not just the visual part. The sound of those heart wrenching screams made it all the more horrendous.

There was no way I was going to give in this time. But I could not have stood the sight.

I cornered Mr Ashish and said, "Sir, I believe it would be best if I leave. I really can't stand this man's voice."

Mr Ashish said "sure" and hurried back to the scene.

The sight had gotten completely unbearable. I had to choose between losing consciousness and leaving so I chose to leave. Had I lost consciousness, I would have ended up adding to the chaos rather than subtracting from it.

I went outside and told a bus to drop me to my room. The driver was surprised enough to see me. He could have said no but he didn't. The Female kind was a rare sight in those areas. And I did not look too well either. Denying was not really an option for him.

I reached home and I wanted to do nothing.

I took a shower and realized that this was the lowest I had been in my life. What was I doing here? On a Friday evening I should have been roaming around in Select City Mall in Saket in Delhi choosing between a micro mini and a mini. I should have had a gorgeous boyfriend with Greek God body by now. Instead of seeing his naked torso, I was seeing stuff horror movies are made of.

It was the first time that even my biggest defence to myself gave away. Even telling myself that I am the daughter of an IAS officer did not feel adequate. This simple trick had worked each and every time since childhood. But today, having seen more than what I had signed up for, I wasn't sure that whether being an IAS officer's daughter prepares you for gory stuff like this.

My second biggest defence to myself was that only very weak people cry and that I am not weak. I had no recollection of the last time I had cried. That day although, I cried out loud and my voice must have echoed in the corridors like that of the man who fell in the acid. Tears rolled down my cheeks like Rohan's mother, the guy who had had a heart attack at the age of twenty five. I felt I was in great pain like that man must have been with his arm in the conveyor belt.

I felt as if I was not going to make the night, as if something within me was eating me up from within. I wanted to be teleported to some other place. There was no way I could stay here any longer.

I went to my balcony and looked at the road. I was four hundred kilometres from any sort of city life. Moreover, in a place where a woman can't even go to the market alone, going to the city alone would almost definitely be disastrous. This plant was my world now.

The best I could do was to ensure human company. I considered my options. I had been acquainted with some women in the hostel. They were definitely not meant for this moment. Back in B school I would have had many options but not anymore.

Amit had seemed too unpleasant a human being for this moment. I was so sure he would not be able to muster up anything better than "everything will be OK" on hearing the situation.

My only option was Malappa. He had the ability to lift your spirits when they were down. I dialled his number.

"Hey, Malappa. Where are you?" I asked. The background was extremely noisy. He was obviously sitting in the Steel Plant.

"Hey! I am here at the Blast Furnace. I had an evening shift today."

"Oh… okay."

The disappointment in my voice made it obvious that I had been hoping that Malappa would be in the township and I wanted to see him.

"Why don't you come over? Just go to the travel desk and ask for a car till the Blast Furnace. Give me a call when you are here."

"Hmm… okay," I said.

Though I said that, I still wasn't sure if I was going to see him or not. But then, I really didn't have any option. I had to go and see him. If I were to sit alone in my room in this state, I could have very easily imploded.

I had been to the Blast Furnace before.

I was stopped at the entrance and was given a helmet and a denim jacket as a safety measure. The mention of the word safety made me feel strange. I put the helmet and the denim jacket on. The environment in the plant was depressing enough in itself and wearing a hideous denim jacket and a helmet at fifty degrees Celsius made matters much worse.

I remembered reading somewhere that denim jackets and jeans were initially designed as a part of plant safety. They are sturdier and can withstand heat in a better way. But there onwards it caught up as a fashion statement and became a global hit that it is today.

I entered the plant and tried to look for Malappa. I was not in a mood to be stared at and hence tried to avoid being seen.

Finally I saw Malappa working in the plant. Even though everybody there followed each and every safety norm, the moment I saw Malappa I could see what a rebel he was. He was working shirtless in the plant. Some other employee would have got a scolding for such behaviour but Malappa was a star employee who was not the kind to play quiet audience to anybody.

Someone must have told him, "You have to wear the denim jacket."

To this, he must have shot back "If the molten metal falls on me then this jacket and helmet would be of no use."

You cannot respond to a retort like that, especially if it comes with as much condescension as Malappa is capable of.

It might not have surprised me as much, had Malappa not been wearing only the denim jacket or just the helmet. But Malappa was working at the plant with nothing but his jeans and his safety boots. He was working topless, without his shirt amongst a bunch of equals who were wearing a formal shirt and a denim jacket over it. Malappa did not give a damn about the rules.

He was working with molten iron, coming out of the furnace. I was now mentally conditioned to not break the safety rules I had been fed all week. I could not have gone close to the point where he was working. Moreover, I was worried about the blemishes my skin could suffer with if I ventured any near that burning inferno of a furnace.

I tried to catch his attention from a distance, as close to the furnace as I could get. He indicated that he needed five minutes to come and see me.

I took a chair at a safe distance and settled down. I had a clear view of Malappa working with the molten metal. He opened the gates at the bottom of the furnace and golden molten metal flowed out. The temperature of the place shot up immediately.

The molten metal looked like molten lava flowing out of a volcano. It was spectacular sight indeed.

But what I saw next was even more spectacular. Malappa had had a rod in his hand to handle the equipment and was hard at work. Although I had noticed on many occasions that Malappa had a good physique, it was only under the golden sheen of the molten metal that I saw the gorgeous cuts on his glistening chiselled body.

Years of physical labour at high temperatures combined with non-junky diet had toned his body and his physique was just like his job: made of steel. He had a whole set of abs and before I realized what was happening, I was dizzyingly smitten. This pleasant sight coming at an unexpected time and the ever mounting frustration had combined to give me a weird cocktail of emotions that I had completely forgotten. I was seduced.

I had allowed myself to be seduced. It was more important

to be sane than being morally correct at that time. And I felt that if I did not make myself feel any better, sanity could have easily become a challenge for me.

He had a dinner break at ten o'clock. There were still ten more minutes to ten o'clock. I kept staring at him for those ten minutes and I could feel my spirits taking an upward curve.

At sharp ten, Malappa dropped the rod in his hand. He put on his shirt and came to see me.

He smiled and said Hi. Our eyes met and I saw realisation dawn in his eyes as he saw me. It was as if he knew what I had been thinking all the while he was working and hence had clearly interpreted the dazed look in my eyes. I wish I could have seen the look in my eyes at that moment. Because whatever it was, I knew Malappa had understood every word of what I wanted to say. I did not have to utter a word.

That look had said much more than anything I could have voiced. For a second, Malappa considered holding my hand and leading me out but a steel plant is hardly a place to hold a woman's hand. He asked me to follow him and I did. He took me to a corner where the next person in sight was at least a hundred meters away. In the dark, there was no way we could have been visible to them.

I looked around to see where we were exactly. Malappa had brought me in the middle of the steel slabs. Molten iron was laden into steel casts and was given cuboidal shapes and then laid one beside the other. Malappa took me to the centre of these slabs. Nobody could have possibly seen us or could have come there.

We had not exchanged a single word since he had said Hi. All the conversations were silent. I was breathing lust and I was looking it.

Malappa pushed me and my back was now touching the steel slab. He moved his head forward to touch my lips with his but I immediately pulled my head back, purely by impulse. It was weird to be doing this. I had never kissed a guy without having exchanged a single word in the day. And I had kissed my share of guys.

But I believed touching his lips would alleviate this feeling of uneasiness that had not left me for a week now. I wanted to feel normal. Touching his lips with mine was supposed to put a lot of things to the back of my head. I was supposed to feel better.

Our lips did come in contact the second time he motioned his head forward to touch my lips. But it was an absolute anticlimax. The fire that I had been breathing did not really wash us over with a burning sensation, the way I had been hoping.

He bit my lips all over. It was the moment. There was no chance of a soft or sensuous kiss. The teeth were going to play a prominent role. I decided to let him bite my lips. I thought the physical pain that Mallapa was inflicting on me would somehow help me forget the mental pain that was weighing me down. Malappa was a violent kisser. Or maybe it was the moment or the setting that a soft kiss would have seemed so out of place.

But even the scratches on my lips did not serve the purpose they were supposed to fulfil. The restlessness and the upheaval within had still not settled down. I was still as unsettled as I had been before I had come.

Malappa's hands were now getting explorative. I felt his hands on my back and they were travelling further. They started from my lower back and travelled upwards on my back. They started traversing my back and motioned to the front. I was sure where they were heading. My heart was beating at a rate, I wondered if it could be heard over the blast furnace.

Would the next step make me feel any better? Would that mark the end of this emotional upheaval that I had been going through? I was going through a tumult of emotions and kissing Malappa had turned out to be such a let-down that I wasn't so sure any more. I was now coming back to my senses.

This was going to stop here. I held Malappa's hands and stopped them there and then. Yet, no words were exchanged.

I motioned to leave but Malappa held my hand.

"It's ok if we don't kiss. But at least let's sit and talk. I like the feel of this place. So noisy and yet so silent," he said.

We sat down where we had been standing. I was not in a mood to speak. It was going to be a monologue from Malappa's side tonight.

"When I initially came here Saumya, I was hoping people here, would be less stupid than Tata Steel," Malappa said.

"But it seems that they are all from the same breed. Everybody is an idiot. It takes me hours to explain simple things to them. This man Manjunath they call my boss, is the biggest idiot of them all. He doesn't know anything at all. We guys are in constant argument over petty things. The fact that hurts him the most is that all the employees listen to me more diligently than they listen to him. I am already diluting his authority in this place."

I liked the feeling of being an effortless listener to what Malappa was speaking. He did not expect a reaction and I did not offer any.

"Manjunath has serious insecurity issues with me. Moreover these stupid rules. There is no logic whatsoever. The worst part is that my boss loves these rules like these rules are his girlfriend. I can totally see what is going to happen here again. I might win The Best Employee Award but my boss is going to hate me from the bottom of his heart."

I nodded. Some more time into Malappa's monologue, resulted in, he and I getting cosy. I liked the feeling a lot. I liked his touch and the firmness of every part of his body.

At around eleven o'clock, Malappa told me that he had to get back to work. As we were exiting, Malappa's boss crossed our path. He made no effort to conceal his surprise and his disapproval of my presence in that place. Thankfully, I was beginning to get used to all sorts of stares. But the lust in his boss's eyes was unprecedented. His boss was reeking hatefulness. His eyes fell on me and pierced through my clothes. I had begun to believe I was inured to such stares now. But this guy was just too cheap.

I left the plant in a better mood. I was feeling marginally better. Good things did happen. I had two days of weekend by myself to get life into perspective once again.

I had decided to spend the weekend by cooking for myself. If the meal on Saturday lunch turned out to be edible, I would invite Vaibhav, Amit and Malappa for dinner in my room. Or maybe we could forget Amit and Vaibhav. That would mean Malappa and I would have dinner together.

I slept better than night. There was still hope.

Chapter 12
The Impurity in the Blast Furnace

I was woken up in the middle of the night by a call from Mr Ashish Rao. I checked the time before picking the call. It was three o'clock. The first time I was sleeping well in the week without sedatives and that too, was disturbed by work. I took a deep gulp to sound less sleepy to Mr Ashish.

"Hello?"

"Hi Saumya. There has been a case and I want you to be there with me. I will just come and pick you up from your accommodation. I will tell you the details on our way. Should I pick you in ten minutes?"

"Hmm... okay sir."

He hung up. So this was going to be another facet of my job. I would be woken up in the middle of the night and shown things which would make me faint.

Mr Ashish stopped his car outside my accommodation and started filling me on the details.

"One of the employees got into a fight with his boss tonight around midnight. The fight got really bad and the boss took a drastic step."

"Oh, you mean he beat him to death?"

"No. It was worse. The boss, along with some allies, threw the person into the Blast Furnace."

"*What?*"

"Yeah. The boss has thrown the person in the Blast Furnace."

"What do you mean *thrown*? How can somebody just throw someone into a furnace?" I asked.

"They took the guy to the top of the furnace. Every furnace has some open space on the top. They took him there and just threw him inside."

"But how can anyone be that gruesome…?"

"I know. That is the most gruesome death anyone can ever get. Sometimes even after all these years of experience, even I am amazed at the kind of incidents one has to see here in the plant."

"So what happened to the body?" I asked.

"There is no body. It has got dissolved in the iron," Mr Ashish, a little too plainly for my comfort.

I was supposed to get used to such stories. They were supposed to rattle me lesser and lesser. And slowly, I was supposed to reach Mr Ashish's stage when I would treat these incidents as if they were a part of life.

But until now, I saw no improvement in the way I would take such stories. And I won't even have the advantage of being completely alert right now because of being half sleepy. I wanted to ask Mr Ashish to turn around and drop me back to my room. I wanted to tell him that I was not being groomed the way he had envisioned me and it was not heading anywhere.

"Nothing was found of the fellow? Not even a bone?"

Mr Ashish shook his head.

So I will not have to look at a charred dead body or any other gory body part today, I thought.

"The boss is in police custody and I think he is gone for life. His alliances would go for five years each at least. There is more than enough evidence against them. There may be press to report the incident in the plant as well."

Mr Ashish drove along until we reached the plant. He parked the car in the middle of the entrance. There was no need of an ambulance because there was nothing to take. Once he parked the car I realized which part of the plant we were in. It was the same Blast Furnace which I had visited only a few hours ago to meet Malappa.

I reached the place and realized that the Blast Furnace had continued working in spite of the incident. There were more people in the plant than usual. Where I was standing two young engineers were standing.

One of the engineers said to the other "When did this happen?"

"Two hours ago," the other replied.

"The body must have reduced to impurities in the steel making process." And both of them broke into a restrained laugh.

"Yeah and he must have shot up the carbon content of the steel as well."

This time around both of them laughed louder but checked themselves soon.

"Or may be the boss had run out of carbon to be added. So he added this guy to increase the carbon content."

This time they could not check themselves.

Somebody's death was a joke for these guys. Deaths were too common a phenomenon for these people to be bothered. I couldn't take it. I wanted to speak to these people.

"I don't think you people should joke about this," I said, approaching them.

The two were taken aback. Firstly, seeing a girl at this hour in that place was strange enough. And being approached by her was even stranger.

They got hold of their surprise and then spoke up.

"All this is a part of our lives, Madam. I have been working in this plant for fifteen years and I know that in each and every accident, it is the worker himself who is making the mistake."

"But in this case, he was pushed into the furnace..." I said.

"That is only half the story madam. Everyone knows that he had got a girl to the plant last night. Who bloody gets a girl to a Blast Furnace? His boss saw him and an altercation ensued."

It then struck me. Malappa had had a tussle with his boss. I had seen extreme hatred and anger in his boss's eyes just the same night.

"What is the name of the victim?" I asked suddenly feeling the place closing on me.

"He was a new recruit from Tata Steel. He had just joined

recently. His name was Malappa."

There was no moment of denial when I got the news. A shriek escaped my mouth immediately. The horrifying thought had crossed my mind and I had been praying already that it would be untrue. It had turned out to be true. In Toranagallu, death can hit you anytime, anywhere.

Standing there, looking at those men, I puked. I succumbed to the constant feeling in the pit of my stomach and let it go. I imagined Malappa falling into the burning metal and my head started whizzing.

Scary visualizations clouded my mind. The mental images of the man falling in the acid came crashing back. Just that that stranger who had drowned was replaced by Malappa in my mind's eye. And the transparent, watery acid was replaced by golden shining molten iron.

I pictured Malappa shrieking in the same way as he must have fell. And then writhing in pain like that guy.

As I stood there, having just heard the news, my thoughts became discrete packets of ideas coming one after the other. One thought was not leading onto the next. Everything around me became hazy. I fainted the second time in seven days and fell like a bundle of mass.

I have only a faint recollection of what happened thereafter. Somebody suggested lifting my legs in the air, as I lay on the grass, to make the blood flow into my head. But I didn't gain complete consciousness until I was in the hospital. I was given a glucose drip and some medicine.

But I knew there was nothing wrong with my body. It was just the extreme depression that I was going through. If I had been messed up till now, it was going to get much worse.

My head was a crowded place. I wondered if this was what they called insanity. I really wanted to talk but there was no Malappa anymore.

He was not there anymore. The thought just kept striking me again and again.

I wanted to shout out. Will the bad things please stop happening. I decided that at the first chance that I will get, I will run.

After a sedative induced sleep, I was discharged the next morning.

I was in a terrible shock from the news. I could almost not fathom what I was seeing around me. But still, I knew I was the only real friend Malappa ever had.

A condolence meeting was arranged on the next day in the hall of the Township. I arranged for a *panditji* to carry out a prayer. Not many people turned up for the prayer.

I was in a particularly bad condition. I would hold strong for a few minutes but then some particular memory of Malappa would strike me and I would break down once again.

Chapter 13
His Side

Two days later, as I was sitting in office, my intercom rang.

"Is this Ms. Saumya Kapoor?"

"Yes."

"There is someone to see you at the company reception. Please come."

I got up and left for the reception.

When I reached there, I was taken aback. For a moment I thought, it was Malappa standing in front of me. But I soon realized it was his elder brother.

"Hi Saumya. I am Malappa's brother. I had come to pick his belongings. So I thought I would come and say Hi."

"Hello," I said.

And then there was an awkward silence.

"I hope you are not facing any problem in collecting the compensation money from the company," I asked.

"No, nothing of that sort," he replied.

Malappa's brother was a strong and stolid man. On his face,

he managed to show no emotion.

I called for a company cab and I escorted him to Malappa's room. This was where he began to get weak. Seeing Malappa's stuff must have ignited memories associated with Malappa in his mind. I decided to leave him alone in this private moment and myself silently cried standing in the corridor.

He came out a few minutes later.

"He was a good guy. It shouldn't have happened to him," he said. I didn't say anything, even though I really agreed.

"He used to talk a lot about you," he said.

"About me?"

"Yeah. I thought you would know that."

"What did he say?" I asked.

"You seem as if you didn't expect this?"

"No, I had no idea."

"So you had no idea that Malappa really liked you?"

"What!"

"I thought you would know..." he said.

"No! He never said anything like that," I said.

"I know... But I thought you would soon have sensed that. From the way he talks and the way he looked at you. I thought girls could do those sort of things."

"Normally I can, but with Malappa, I had no clue."

"I know. Malappa was good at concealing everything."

I fell silent even though there were a thousand things I wanted to ask him at that moment.

What did he say about me? When did he talk about me? Any incidents he might have told him?

But I decided against asking him. He must be in as much shock as me. I spared him the torture.

He packed all the stuff he wanted to take and left late in the afternoon.

During my evening walk, I looked at the running plant in front of the township. I realized that death was such an anticlimax in this place. Dying people were a part and parcel of this location. Definitely, I did not fit here.

Standing there, the thought of quitting this job and this city crossed my mind. Too many horrifying memories were now associated with this place for me to stay on. A change of profile or department was not going to be enough. I needed a different world altogether. There was nothing left to discuss or ponder about the topic. It was an obvious fact. I had to leave at the first chance I would get.

PART 3: Three Months Have One Day More Than 90 Days

Chapter 14
When I Start Reverse Counting Till Ninety

On Monday morning, I told Mr Ashish that I was quitting. He wasn't surprised. In fact, it was evident that he had expected this.

"I guess we should start your notice period straight away," he said.

"Sure sir. And how long would that be?"

"According to the company policy, it will be three months long," he said.

He had a look of concern on his face. He understood that spending three more months at this place would be a daunting task for me.

"Okay, sir. So if my notice period starts now, I can leave on the last day of September right?"

"Yes, Saumya. What department would you like to work in for these three months?"

"I think HR Department would be alright. I might gain some important exposure before I join my next job."

"Sure. I would fix you a meeting with the Head of

Department in the HR this afternoon. He would carve out a project for you, I am sure," said Mr Ashish. He was a sweet guy.

I reached back to my room and hung a calendar on my wall. I crossed the date and started my countdown of three months. I counted that these three months were ninety one days. I lay down on my bed for the night and started watching the good old F.R.I.E.N.D.S on my laptop to kill time. I slept off during the eighth episode of the night.

It was at seven o'clock in the morning that my phone rang. It was from an unknown Toranagallu number.

My brain automatically assumed that there was yet another accident somewhere in some part of the plant. I had every reason to be upset this time. I was expecting it to be Mr Ashish Rao on the other side.

"Hello Saumya madam?" It was not Mr Ashish, but some stranger.

"Yes?"

"I am calling from the gate security here at the residential complex. Our senior is asking you to come here. It is seriously urgent."

"Can I know what is this regarding?"

"No madam. You just have to come."

"Hmm. Ok."

I brushed my teeth and got into a pair of jeans. A crowd was waiting for me at the entrance of the residential complex.

"Saumya madam?"

"Yes?" I said.

The crowd thinned a little as I walked towards it. The people moved apart to show something on the road. A man was lying on the road and the crowd around him was looking at him as if he was a homeless beggar who had walked into the Lala Steel premises.

The security walked up to me and said hello.

"Saumya madam," he said. "Sorry to have disturbed you so early in the morning. This mad man walked into the Lala Steel premises last night. We found him in the drain this morning. He is stinking so bad... I think he has had loads of beer with an overdose of some drug. The reason we have called you is because we have found this paper in his pocket."

The paper had my name, my phone number and my address written in my own handwriting. I had no clue what this meant.

Who was he?

I walked closer to the man lying on the road and saw his face. It was Shubhro.

I checked the date on my watch and I realized it had been a

month since I had met him. That meant that he had completed his three months at Hampi. As per his move on theory, he had moved on from Hampi and come to Toranagallu for the next three months.

"I know him," I told the security guard. "Arrange for an ambulance to take him to the hospital".

Chapter 15
When I Restart Reverse Counting Till Ninety

What followed was yet another day in the hospital. Having seen so much in the last week, Shubhro's unconsciousness perturbed me no more than a scratch on the arm. Too much beer with some weed must have thrown him off balance and into the drain.

It had worked for him. He had managed to reach me, one way or the other, in better condition or worse. The familiar sight of the hospital once again. I dialled Mr Ashish's phone and told him that I needed the day off. I explained to him that one of my old friends had met with an accident in the residential complex.

"But if you are taking care of him, aren't you doing your job anyway? Then how is it an off day? You *are* actually working by being there."

I smiled and hung up. It meant I would be marked present for this day.

The doctors told me he would take two hours to gain consciousness. I went out of the hospital premises and lit up a cigarette. I realized I was more relaxed in this hospital set up than I might have been in my bedroom.

∽

Two hours later, I saw Shubhro walking out of his room. The nurse was shocked to see him walk. He was supposed to be getting a glucose drip and stick to the bed for a day. Instead he had gained consciousness to find the glucose drip on his hand. His instant reaction was to pull the needle out from his arm and walk out of the room.

I smiled on seeing him. He really did look like a homeless beggar as he walked out. He was a good ten meters away from me but he carried the extremely strong smell of the drain with him. He had not had a haircut for some time and his hair was all over the place. His shirt had not been washed for at least a few weeks or maybe it was the fall in the drain. He was a pitiable sight.

But he seemed completely at ease with his ugliness. In fact, he seemed to be relishing it.

The nurse rushed to him and took him inside the room. I followed the two of them.

"Here take this soap and this shampoo, you dirty fellow and rub yourself clean," the nurse told Shubhro.

Shubhro grinned and took the soap and the shampoo and the towel. His grin was so cute… that is if you ignored the smell coming from his mouth.. He hadn't brushed for a few days.

He went to the bathroom in the hospital as I waited in the

waiting room for him to come out. An hour later, he walked out with a towel wrapped around his body. The nurse gave him a hospital gown to be worn.

His features had now come through the shadows of dirt and dust to shine in full glory. His dark black piercing eyes and black hair were back to their natural colours and quality. He looked refined as if he hadn't touched anything dirty for a long time.

I looked at him and thought that in spite of being an Indian, he was yet so foreign. He looked Bengali only when he told you that he is Bengali. I mean, his body was Bengali but his clothes, demeanour or behaviour was light years from being Bengali, or even Indian. He was living a maverick's life and had gotten over the rat race.

In a rat race, even if you win, you are still a rat.

Shubhro walked up to me with a sheepish smile and said "Do you get shirts and jeans in your Toragallum?"

"It is Toranagallu."

"Toragallum?"

"To – ra – na – ga – llu."

"To – ra – na – gallu," Shubhro said and smiled, with a spark in his eye. He was cute.

"What did you say you wanted?"

"Clothes. I haven't brought any along."

Shopping could not possibly have been a huge task in Toranagallu. If you wanted a pair of jeans, you had to choose between the only two options available at the Departmental

Store. One of them was blue and the other was black. I bought one of each for Shubhro. I bought three T-shirts for him as well. And undergarments. It felt terrible to be buying guys' underwear. I felt as if I was a mother already.

He insisted on being discharged the same evening and the doctor agreed on my insistence.

The next question was where he was going to stay. I called up the Hospitality Department and booked a room for him. The room rent was Rs. five hundred a day. The same room in Delhi would have cost five thousand. But still, five hundred rupees a day is quite unaffordable, especially if he was planning to stay for three months.

Shubhro had been discharged from the hospital after the shower. He got into the ugly clothes that I had brought him and made them look good. This guy could transform the way jeans and T-shirts looked.

We took a lift from a truck carrying iron ore to go from the hospital to the township, the residential area. Sitting in the truck with Shubhro, the same thought crossed my mind yet again.

"You are from Delhi, aren't you?" Shubhro asked.

"Yup."

"So how does it feel?"

"How does what feel?" I asked.

"*This.* Sitting in a truck, being driven by a non-Hindi speaker, with an Indian hippie, and that too in *Toranagallu?* How does it feel?"

"What do you think? Obviously, it feels terrible!"

"Oh no, I know it feels great. It's just that you don't know that it feels great," Shubhro said.

Shubhro had this I-know-all and yet-I-am-not-cocky feel about him. His innocent face helped him pull off all things.

"Shut up, Shubhro."

"See, Delhi would have been so boring. There would have been too much sameness in your days. Here, every day is different. You can live the Delhi life whenever you want. But *this*, this won't come back."

That was one very positive way to look at it. But you had to be a very positive person like Shubhro to look at it which I wasn't.

I was quiet which meant that Shubhro had definitely got me thinking.

"And where would I be staying?" Shubhro asked.

"In the guest house, obviously," I said.

Shubhro winced. "But I thought we would be flatmates?"

"What? I don't have a flat? I just have a room!" I exclaimed.

"Oh okay. But if you had a flat you would have let me stay right?" He was trying to be cheeky.

"No way. Living with somebody as dirty as you under the same roof? No way!"

"So if I would mend my ways and you had a flat, would you let me stay with you?" He was acting cute and being successful at it.

"Go to hell, Shubhro. You are a bloody drunkard hippie, the last type that I would like to trust in the world. I would never let you enter my house, leave alone live in it."

I was trying to be soft yet firm. I did not want him to get wrong signals. I knew he had had his ways with the women during his travels and wanted to clarify from the first day itself that I wasn't willing to be one of them. It would have been easier had he been worse looking.

He smiled at my retort as if he had spotted a weakness in my responses. And yet, I could not have been firmer.

On our way, we crossed the Lala Steel Bar. His tongue hung out on seeing the bar. On our way back from the hospital, this fellow wanted to have more beer. It was time I clarified a few things with him.

"See Shubhro, it is because of me that you are looking human after what you were looking in the morning. You should have seen yourself. The dirtiest, stinkiest pig in the world would have looked cleaner than you. Now that you are living here, you would have to live by my rules or you are welcome to go anytime."

My manners were teacher-ly but it worked. Shubhro was listening with intent to my orders.

"You would have to quit weed altogether as long as you are staying here. I am responsible for keeping you here. Any sort of misbehaviour from your side would reflect on me as well."

Shubhro nodded. I hadn't expected this to be so easy. He was listening to me! And he looked so cute when he did.

"And you would have to quit beer or any form of alcohol till you are here—" I said.

But he cut me in between. This was expectedly too much for him to take "You have got to be kidding. Even if I *want* to quit alcohol, my body can*not* quit. It will start showing withdrawal symptoms and I will not last till the seventh day."

He was literally defensive as if I had said the stupidest thing in the world.

"Ok then! You can drink once every week but not more than that," I conceded.

He seemed desperate to make this work the way I wanted. He agreed to this as well.

"Ok. I will not have beer more than once a week but even I have a condition. Whenever I will get drunk, you will also get drunk with me unless of course, you have some important work."

I did not exactly say yes but the cuteness of the demand made me smile. That was an even stronger confirmation than a yes.

I might have stopped here but he himself asked "Anything else?"

I said, "Yes. You would have to bathe every day and shave at least twice every week. People will see me with you. Your personality will be a part of my personality."

He laughed out loud at this. He thought it was funny.

"You know, in my three years of travelling, I have lived with a lot of people with very different beliefs. People have asked me to do the previous two things as you have. But the third thing you have stated is something completely new to me."

"You probably didn't meet anyone clean enough."

"I know! Isn't this the best place ever? Walking around with a hunk who has hippie written on his face can prove damaging to your image for sure. And you know whenever anyone has asked me even for the first two of your requests, I have shoved it away as if it was an absolute impossibility. I have never agreed to any one of them even once. But today, when you ask me to do it, I feel like giving it a shot. I want to do it for you."

This time he smiled an innocent smile, as if he was telling me that he liked me and was not being comfortable telling me so. In a way, he was telling me he would do something for me he had not done for anyone. In a way he was telling me that he did like me.

There was one more thing I had wanted to ask of him. I wanted to tell him to not be hopeful of any sex or action from me. Shubhro had had his ways with women during his travels and with a face like his, it was completely understandable. But there was no way I would get involved with somebody who I would never see again after ninety days. He was welcome to stay in the same township but every time he would try to make a move, I would turn it down with equal conviction.

Giving into temptation would only lead to depression on the ninety first day. I had had my share of depression and was going to avoid all such sources.

We had dinner together. When I had lived in the B school hostel, I had taken a lot of things for granted. One of them was good company over dinner. Every night I had sat with my friends who entertained me and vice versa without realizing that what a tedious task it could become to arrange for a good conversation over dinner.

Shubhro could have been nice company for dinner even if he was sitting on the table with his mouth shut but a smile pasted across his face. You could have just looked at him and felt that you were having a great conversation.

But he was not the type to sit quietly. He was the type who had a story for every occasion. And every story would be based in a different city, with a different set of friends and with a completely new moral in the end. And the morals were certainly not the kinds one would find in a moral science book.

"Beer is great for health."

"Weed is a one stop solution to every problem in the world."

"Whenever you have a choice between fucking and not fucking, go ahead and fuck."

Not a sentence he uttered was ever boring. I could have liked a man with even one of those experiences in his kitty and here Shubhro was, sitting in front me, with a plethora of them. The fact that I was so disoriented in life made me all the more vulnerable. I had every reason to be so.

He taught me how to use a pair of chopsticks over dinner but I failed terribly.

Post dinner, we went for a walk. The wind was always a few miles faster in the open spaces of Toranagallu. After around an hour, we completely ran out of conversation and walked silently. The thing about silences is that they make me reflect back on the past every time.

Only seventeen days ago, I had slept in my own bedroom in Delhi in my shorts. I was oblivious to the Steel Making

Process and the whole process of what is to be done if somebody dies while making it. I was happy to watch a Shah Rukh Khan Movie trailer and was sad only when his woman died in the movie.

So much had happened in the last two weeks. And how much had my perspective changed in life.

Shubhro must have been lost in his own set of thoughts. But I was sure his outlook must have been more future oriented than mine. He must have been busy thinking how the next three months were going to shape. From what I knew of him, he might have been wondering if he can kiss me today.

He did not try to kiss me that day. He dropped me to my building and left for his own.

I went back to my room and saw the calendar in my room. I saw the day's date and made a note of it.

I took a pen and above the date on the calendar, I wrote 'First Day with Shubhro'.

I looked at the calendar and tried to calculate the day when Shubhro would be leaving. It would be the day before the last day of September. That was one day before I was supposed to leave Toranagallu for good.

The previous day I had calculated the day my notice period would get over and it had come out to be the last day of September. Apparently, the course my life would take had summed up in these two days.

(I realised that the calculations that I had done on these two days decided how I would live my life for the next three months.)

Chapter 16
The Fourth Day with Shubhro

When I reached home on the fourth evening, I could see that Shubhro wasn't his loose and carefree self. There was a hint of irritation on his face. I hadn't seen this side of him. I had expected that he would get bored of Toranagallu very fast but the whine on his face on just the fourth day of his stay was way sooner than I had expected. Or maybe it was the absence of weed and beer that was getting on his nerve.

Or the women.

"What happened, Shubhro? Why is there a whine on your face?" I asked at the first chance that I got.

"I am too bored," he said.

"Hmm."

"I should make some friends. Where is the guy you brought to Hampi? What was his name? Mapalla?"

"Malappa."

The mention of Malappa's name froze my blood in a weird way. I still did not have the strength to narrate the story to him. I would have to relive it if I had to do that.

I noticed that Shubhro was looking at me with intent. He was trying to read my reaction and he noticed something was not okay. He realized it and didn't try to push this topic any further.

"Well, it's just that I am not used to this. It is damn tough to sit in the guest house all day and do nothing. Normally, I would have a few people to chat with and spend the day. But this place is just too dead. This place is damn suffocating. I need to start doing something, Saumya."

I felt better as Malappa's topic passed.

"Doing something? What do you mean by doing something? And what can a useless drunkard like you even do?" I joked. Shubhro took it well. I always knew that he took great pride in his uselessness.

"I haven't done anything for years... But now I think I need to start doing something. Maybe you can give me some of your work. Maybe I can help you. Or maybe get a job in your company."

Shubhro's tone had gotten desperate. I could now understand how bored he must have got. But he was too unreliable a person to tag along to office. It wasn't like he won't be noticed either. Wherever he would go he was bound to be noticed.

"Take you to office? You are kidding, right? How can you possibly be working at Lala Steel?"

"I will do anything Saumya. Anything is better than just sitting in the guest house all day long. To be honest, I am not even looking for any salary or stipend. I just want work."

"I understand... but what *can* you do?" I said.

"Let's do one thing. I have read about the social service being done by Lala Steel. Can you introduce me to the social service team at Lala Steel? I will work with them. I don't even want a salary. I know they always need people there."

"But why are you doing this, Shubhro? You are not that kind of a person. You are an MBA in Finance. You can do so many other things in life. Why do you want to do something like that?"

Shubhro was taken aback. He hadn't expected such a sharp opposition from me. But I was genuinely baffled by his decision.

"See Saumya, look at it like this. For me, it is impossible to sit idle for the whole day. I have to start doing something to turn the day into the night. Normally I would have a bunch of ten fifteen co-travellers who would help me in doing so. But here, I've got absolutely nothing to do."

"I know."

"In such a situation, I have to think of the least meaningless job I can do. And helping the poor should definitely be the least meaningless thing I can think of. Trust me, it will be the easiest way to tolerate these three months helping the poor."

I looked at Shubhro and almost waited for him to break into a laugh. Such stuff coming from him was just plain funny.

But then I did consider taking him to see Laxmi ma'am. I began thinking that Shubhro would definitely be easy to explain to the social service team and that telling the team that he was a friend from Kolkata who had come because he wanted to help the people in Karnataka would be quite believable. I decided to give it a shot.

I promised Shubhro that I would definitely see what I could do for him, given that the task of introducing him to the social service team at Lala Steel, not be too tough. I was certain that they would definitely get him involved into something productive. I also toyed with the idea of telling them that he was an MBA in Finance and that they could use his skills to their advantage. The fact that Shubhro was flexible about the work would be in his favour.

Chapter 17
The Fifth Day with Shubhro

Shubhro got up very early that day. He also shaved, combed his hair and dressed up neatly. He looked like a good boy.

I introduced him to Laxmi ma'am. In her twenty year experience in the social service department, she had seen many MBAs who had the fire in their belly to help the poor in rural parts of India. Shubhro fit the bill perfectly. She had no reason to have any sort of doubts.

This was the moment where Shubhro was supposed to voice his requirement of a salary, if there at all was any. Shubhro, having seen so much in life must have known this. I had not expected him to hesitate. The fact that he stayed quiet at this moment implied that he really wasn't looking for any salary.

Moreover, I was sure he was carrying no papers to prove his identity. He might have his passport but I wasn't sure about a bank account.

Why should he? I was going to pay those five hundred rupees a day for his accommodation.

Mrs. Laxmi took him to her office and I left the social service department. I could now go back to lying to people that they could achieve more in life by listening to me.

Chapter 18
The Seventeenth Day with Shubhro

Amit and Vaibhav had become popular enemies. Amit's job was to assist Vaibhav in the training sessions that he conducted. Amit sincerely believed that whatever Vaibhav said in those sessions was utter nonsense. And Vaibhav believed that people did not enjoy the sessions because Amit himself kept an irritated grimace on his face during the sessions which nobody liked.

One day in the team meeting, it got really ugly between the two of them. Both of them wanted to impress the Head of the Department and claim credit for everything that was right.

Eventually Amit mustered up the courage to say, "Vaibhav, you are boring and preachy in your sessions. More people sleep in your sessions than they do in boring lectures."

Vaibhav retorted, "Had it not been for me, nobody would turn up for any of the sessions. People care only for my industry experience of five years. You are a new born Amit. I challenge you to convince five people to listen to you in a session."

It was decided that both would now handle independent

workshops. Vaibhav would have to do it himself while Amit was going to get me as an ally for his workshop. I was anyways jobless after I had quit the Safety Department.

The moment Vaibhav heard this, he sank in his chair. He could see what even Amit and I could not see at that time. Amit's workshops became a total hit. His second session was a house full. People in several plants were pestering their Head of Departments to let them attend his workshop.

As modest as I would like to be, the fact was that Amit's popularity came from my looks rather than his ability.

On the seventeenth day after Shubhro had arrived, Amit and I were taking a session on 'Boss Subordinate Relationship'. In the middle of the session, I got a call from Mr Ashish Rao.

Normally, I would have rejected the call in the middle of a session. But Mr Ashish Rao would call me only in special circumstances. I excused myself to attend the call.

"Hello?" I said. There was a lot of noise where Mr Ashish Rao was standing.

"Hi Saumya. Hey listen, there has been a huge situation here at the entrance of the plant. We are terribly understaffed to handle such a situation. I know you have shifted to Training and Development but if you can spare a few hours here, we guys can save a lot of chaos. It would be great if you can come."

I heard him out and pondered. The reason why I had quit the Safety Department was because of my instability. The seventeen days with Shubhro had stabilized me enough to enable me to lend a helping hand to Mr Ashish for a day. This was something highly doable.

"Sure sir. Where do I see you?"

"I will just come and pick you up. I will give you the details on our way."

Mr Ashish arrived in his gypsy. I remembered the two weeks that I had worked with him. The gypsy was where he briefed me on every situation.

"It's almost a mob there today," he told me once I was settled in the jeep. "One of our trucks lost control today and slammed into a pavement. A few of the villagers were sitting on the pavement. Five of these villagers died instantly. Once the news reached the village, the whole village got agitated against the company. The situation has completely gone out of hand."

"What exactly are they doing sir?" I asked.

"They are throwing stones on our gates. They broke whatever property they could find outside the plant area. One of the employees was driving back home from the plant to the residential complex. They climbed to the top of the car and broke its glasses. Fortunately, the employee was a good driver and he managed to put the car in reverse gear and run away."

The scene definitely seemed scary. "So what is our role going to be in this situation?"

"The situation is pretty bad out there. I would have to talk to the mob and ask them what exactly they want from Lala Steel. The seniors have told me that a compensation of twelve lakhs for the dead ones is highly doable."

I internalised the facts.

As he was saying this, the noise of a mob was getting louder as we approached the plant gate. The sight was scarier that I had thought. The crowd was throwing stones on the gate and inside the plant. The area had been vacated to prevent casualties. The stones were landing within ten meters of where Mr Ashish stopped his car.

"We cannot do anything until the police arrive. We cannot even go close to the gate."

The police arrived within five minutes. The police took another hour to silence the crowds. The Inspector gave the news that it was now safe for Mr Ashish and three people from his team to go and negotiate with the crowd. Mr Ashish seemed worried. In spite of all his years of experience, Lala Steel kept throwing new challenges in front of him.

With such a situation at hand, which book can he refer to?

What precedent can he use to take guidance except his own experience and good sense?

Mr Ashish, Chetan, Pavak and I were supposed to talk to the crowd and settle the deal with them. Mr Ashish was going to be our leader and Chetan, Pavak and I were accompanying him for no apparent reason.

Mr Ashish took the loudspeaker in his hand and addressed the crowd from the gate of Lala Steel. "Whatever has happened today has been most unfortunate. We are truly sorry for the situation. The loss is truly irreparable. But as compensation in exchange of the lost lives, Lala Steel offers a settlement of Rs five lakhs to those who have died."

The moment Mr Ashish said Rs five lakhs, the mob broke into a loud noise. The crowd was not ready to listen to what he had to say. He had no opportunity to negotiate with the crowd.

He made his next offer. "Okay, the final offer from our side is Rs eight lakh to the family of every victim."

The crowd had the same reaction. I realized at this point that it was impossible to negotiate with the whole crowd. When an emotionally charged crowd stands together, they have the power to take on any negotiator in the world.

I asked Mr Ashish Rao to hand over the loudspeaker to me. He had lost his goodwill in front of the crowd. Anything he would have said would have been negatively received by the crowd. The need for a different speaker was immediate and unexplainable.

Mr Ashish Rao was amazed on seeing my reaction but he still conceded and handed over the loudspeaker to me.

I took the loudspeaker, mustered all the courage I had, running in my blood and turned the loudspeaker on.

"Having recently lost a friend to an accident, I understand the pain you people are going through today. The lives that we have lost were truly unfortunate. I even understand your anguish towards this company."

Pause.

"The company mourns the death of these brothers as much as you. The company extends its heartfelt condolences to the family. But what can the company do really?"

Pause.

"The company endeavours to contribute to the cause of making up to the losses of the families of these young men in whichever way they can. For this, we request a representative of you people to come and talk with us so that both sides can present their cases clearly."

What I said was well received. The crowd liked my idea. Negotiating with one person was much more practical than negotiating with the whole mob. The crowd had a ten minute discussion at the end of which a fifty-something man came forward and declared himself as the representative we had demanded.

"Madam, I am the representative you were looking for. My only condition is that I will talk with you and not with this fellow, Ashish Rao. I don't want him to speak in between."

Mr Ashish Rao looked at me. Surely, I was going to answer this question if I was up for this challenge.

Mr Ashish Rao knew that he won't get a chance to give me any tips on negotiation. He quickly came close to me and hurriedly murmured a few instructions in my ears.

"The management has allowed us a maximum of twelve lakhs for every person who has died."

I nodded and quickly wrote the figures on my palm.

The leader of the mob and I sat down in a room. It was just the two of us and a security guard in the room.

Both of us put forward our initial figure for the negotiation.

"Fifteen lakhs," said the leader of the mob.

"Nine lakhs," I said.

A fierce negotiation followed.

"Do you even know how little nine lakhs are? The families

have lost their earning member. Nine lakhs would disappear in less than five years."

I counter argued.

Two hours later, the leader settled for a sum of Rs eleven lakhs for everybody who had died. I saw my palm on which I had written the allowable amounts. The management was willing to pay up till twelve lakh rupees but the leader had settled for eleven lakh rupees.

As we were about to shake hands, I stopped my hand.

"Baba, eleven lakh is good amount, but using the power that I have in my hand, I am allowed to offer you up to twelve lakh rupees. Let the final amount be twelve lakh rupees for the family. For the management, one lakh rupees is nothing. It just means a minor adjustment to their balance sheet. But it can change the lives of these poor villagers."

The leader looked at me with amazement. He raised his palm and kept it on my head. This was his way of blessing me. I felt truly blessed at that moment.

The security guard in the room had also been watching the negotiation. He came forward and shook my hand to express his appreciation. I felt like a hero at that moment. I had just proved myself to the leader and the security guard and also the management. I felt triumphant.

The leader of the mob came out of the negotiation room and asked for a mike. He announced to the crowd that the management had had to bend their knees to our demands. They had had to offer twelve lakh rupees to every family that had lost a son today.

Had Mr Ashish Rao offered the crowd Rs twelve lakh, the crowd would have considered it a useless amount. But when their leader announced the same in such an emphatic manner, the same amount seemed like a victory.

The leader came up to me and thanked me again before he left. The mob had dispersed with in fifteen minutes.

"What next, sir?" I asked Mr Ashish Rao once the situation was over.

"I have to take you to the management and tell them what you have done," he said and smiled.

Chapter 19
Be Your Friend's Envy

It was eleven o'clock in the night when Mr Ashish dropped me in front of my building. I picked up my phone and wondered whether I should call up Shubhro. I decided against it and kept the phone back.

I looked around my room and realized I was terribly conversation starved. I picked the phone again and called up Shubhro. I told him to come over to my place. I also told him to get some food packed on his way.

Shubhro was going to take at least half an hour to reach with the food. I thought I would video call Vartika in the meantime through Skype. I messaged Vartika to come online.

Vartika took another ten minutes to come. I turned on the video. Vartika was sitting in her bedroom in a noodle strap top and shorts.

"Hey! Shubhro would be coming over in a few minutes. You can cover up if you want when you talk to him," I told her. She was not the type to do so but still informing her was my duty.

"Shubhro? Awesome name! Is he hot? If yes, I might want

to take some clothes off," she joked. I missed her nonsensical humour.

"Yeah he is an absolute eye candy. But you keep your eyes off him. He is my guy," I told her, being possessive.

"Oooooooh! Somebody is in love. And I don't even know."

"There is no love shove—" As I said this, the door opened behind me. Shubhro had arrived with the food. Vartika was on the speaker. Shubhro must have heard what Vartika had just said. Shit.

"Hey! What did you get to eat?" I acted normal as if nothing had happened.

"*Dal* Fry with four chapatis. Your favourite."

It seemed he had not heard it. At least he behaved as if he had heard nothing. That was good enough for me.

"Nice! Come here. Meet Vartika, my friend from MDI. Say Hi."

Shubhro came close to the camera and saw Vartika on the screen.

"Oh, hi Vartika. I must say you are smoking hot."

Vartika and I were equally surprised. The only difference was that she loved it and I hated it. All she needed was a reason to start flirting.

"Wow Shubhro. You are not bad either. Why are you wasting your looks in Toranagallu? Come to Delhi sometime."

"Sure. I will stay at your place when I come to Delhi," Shubhro said.

That meant Shubhro was going to stay at Vartika's place and get drunk. "Once we will be drunk we will do naughty things together."

"Cut it out, the two of you. Vartika I will catch you after dinner. Shubhro must also be quite hungry. Bye!" I said and turned the flap of monitor down. Vartika must have felt insulted but she will be okay after ten minutes. It surely felt good to flaunt Shubhro in front of Vartika. I wish I could have flaunted him in front of everybody.

Vartika had pulled my leg infinite times. When I told her I was getting my legs waxed, she asked what the need for it in Toranagallu was. She had every reason to be fuming.

I had been waiting to tell the whole day's incident to Shubhro. The management and Mr Ashish Rao had shown their share of appreciation. But there was something about hearing a good word from Shubhro. I wondered how it would feel to hear a bravo from him.

He heard silently but did not utter a single word. He just kept indicating that he was listening but that was it. I finished dinner and we chit chatted for a while. I then asked him to leave.

I slept very peacefully that night. There is nothing like making your best friend writhing with jealously and surprising your boss with your ability.

I could have easily been preoccupied with the images of the riot I had witnessed the same evening but thanks to Vartika, I was soon dreaming of walking into The Alumni Meeting at

MDI with Shubhro. I imagined envy painted on the faces of all the girls there and slept with a contented smile on my face..

Chapter 20
The Forty Seventh Day with Shubhro

I had met Sridhar who had had an accident on the road before I had joined the company and all I knew was that the company was somehow responsible his miserable existence. He was a fourteen year old teen from a neighbouring village. I had bandaged and probed into the kind of life that he led and had got to know that at the tender age of fourteen, Sridhar, instead of going to school, struggled to make ends meet and lived on the left over food from the mess plates.

Shubhro and I were taking a walk in the shopping complex in the township after dinner when I bumped into Sridhar. He was truly a son of Karnataka. When I saw him now, he had set up a small shop of South Indian snacks. He had a wheeled cart on which he had set up a gas stove and cooked for his customers.

His face lit up on seeing us. Even I was taken aback on seeing his reaction. Where he had been happy to see me earlier, this time it seemed that he was overjoyed.

I went up to him and as I got closer to him I realized that he had not been looking at me at all. He had been looking at

Shubhro. He was happy to see Shubhro not me.

"Saab, I got the ten thousand rupees through the social service department. This shop was erected on that money. And god promise sir I have already started returning the money as well. Thank you so much for helping me with that loan sir. You changed my life."

Sridhar meant what he said. I could felt the earnest words were coming straight from his heart. He really was very thankful to Shubhro.

"You don't have to thank me, Sridhar. Just work hard, that's enough."

I did not understand. Once we had said bye to Sridhar, I asked Shubhro what that was all about. I realized that I had given such little credit to Shubhro's ability to work that I had never really probed into what he was doing in his unpaid job at the Social Service Department. But today, I did put up the question as we walked towards the artificial lake at Toranagallu.

"I met Sridhar during one of my regular visits to the village. Laxmi ma'am was with me. I asked Sridhar about the kind of life that he leads and was truly touched by his living conditions. Earlier, he used to live on the leftover food in the mess at Toranagallu but then one day, he met with an accident and he stopped coming here."

I told Shubhro about the bandage incident and that I was aware of his condition.

"So the next thing I asked Sridhar was what he would do if I gave him ten thousand rupees. Sridhar wanted to buy a cart and sell *dosas* and *idlis*. I asked him how he planned on implementing the idea and after a heart to heart talk with him it was clear that he was capable of executing the idea. So I ensured I arranged a loan of ten thousand for him. Ten thousand is hardly any money in the long run but it can surely help a family eat two meals a day. It truly did make a difference."

Shubhro was soaked in discomfort as he told this story. He knew that I thought of him as a useless fellow who could never do anything kind or intelligent. Seeing him like this surprised me and I started seeing this useless vagabond in new light. I wondered if Shubhro was doing this out of pure boredom or out of an internal drive to change everything.

I looked at Shubhro and I realised that I had misunderstood him quite a lot . I had never expected him to be capable of empathizing. It seemed he really had been working in the social service department.

I had never been able to fathom this guy completely. There had always been a certain air of mystery about him. With the forty seven days that I had spent with him, I knew that the level of intrigue had been coming down. But suddenly, with this incident, I was back to square number one. There was no way that I knew this guy.

He had the knack of surprising me again and again.

Chapter 21
The Seventy Third Day with Shubhro

Shubhro had proved that he was the most accommodative friend anyone could ever have. He had given up his bad habits on being asked just once and had stuck with his promise diligently. By the seventy third day, he had become a better known person in Toranagallu than I.

It was not because of him being so exotic to the land. It was not even about his looks. It was purely because of his 'never say die' spirit and the kind of talents he had.

It seemed to me that there was no trade that he wasn't a pro at. When the newly recruited Engineers wanted to audition for their Toranagallu band, Shubhro outclassed the guys conducting the audition.

When I asked him, he told me that his friend Mr Anderson in Trinidad and Tobago was the one to have taught him the art. I remembered Shubhro mentioning Mr Anderson when we had gotten drunk together in Hampi.

He told me the women in Brazil loved it when he played the guitar. So he did more and more of it and had gradually practised his way to a level where he could play it very well.

When a poster was put for a team of football, Shubhro was the first one to reach the trials. Nobody on the whole field could touch a ball in his feet.

When I asked he reacted with, "What do you expect? I spent six months with footballers in Brazil."

Every time he offered to cook dinner for me, he proved he was magician.

When I asked, he told me house wives in Peru made the best sex. And food was the best excuse to enter their houses.

When the Chartered Accountants were discussing a problem on the next table in the restaurant, Shubhro went up to them. In five minutes he became a part of the discussion. He ended up becoming a significant part of the solution.

When I asked he told reminded me that he is an MBA from IIM Calcutta.

When a computer went down, he had the skill to bring it back.

When I asked, he told me that Aman, one of the Delhi theatre guys he used to harg around with during his stay in Delhi, was a software engineer and his roommate for a month.

Years of weird exposure had made Shubhro the most useful guy ever.

But what I liked the most about him was that he knew how

to handle me and my moods. Nothing he ever said was out of place.

Nothing he ever said made me feel worse than I had been feeling before he had said it.

He was a masterful talker. Planning an eight hour outing with him seemed comfortable because you know he won't let you get bored. Seventy three days with him had been seventy three days of unadulterated bliss. When I had met him, I was emotionally broken and was feeling the worst I ever had. Not only had he brought me back on my feet, I now felt more stable than ever before.

"So have you slept with a lot of women?" I asked him one fine evening.

"Yeah, more than the usual," he said it so casually that it felt as if he was telling me his favourite choice of bread.

"But you must have broken so many hearts?"

"Well, not really. I had rules. I never told them I love them if I didn't. I never told them that I will be around for long. They always knew that it was a maximum three month thing. And I didn't complain."

That seemed fair enough. It's the lying which is the disgusting part.

"Hmm," I said and Shubhro clicked a picture of my feet and my anklet. He was obsessed with my body parts and would click them over and over again.

Eighteen days were left to finish my notice period of ninety days. Also, if Shubhro was to stick to his belief of moving on in ninety days, then he was supposed to leave in seventeen days.

The fact that these good days were numbered was truly saddening. How I wish Shubhro would junk his belief of moving this one time. How I wish he would stay longer... Forever, if possible.

Chapter 22
The Eighty Fourth Day with Shubhro

Everybody in the company had received the mail from Laxmi ma'am. The social service department had organized a grand lunch for everybody from the management. I did not blame them to have ignored people below the management level. No auditorium could have been large enough to accommodate that many people.

I had not paid much attention at the reason behind the lunch. I had just landed there without having a clue as to why I was there. I always had the excuse of being swamped with work for myself. However it might not have been completely true.

I reached the hall and looked for Shubhro. He was busy welcoming people along with Laxmi ma'am. The banner read that there was a presentation scheduled immediately after lunch. There had been an agenda behind the lunch. The social service department had wanted to say something.

I was surprised to see Shubhro step up to make the presentation instead of Laxmi ma'am. He had become her number one man. He must have done some work worth being noticed to have deserved such an honour.

"Welcome ladies and gentleman to this meeting called by social service department. I am Shubhrodeep Shyamchaudhary. I come from Kolkata.

The objective of this meeting is to inform you of the work we have been doing and inform you of how you can contribute.

For two and a half months, we have been trying to understand how we can change maximum number of lives with our budget of ten crore rupees. How can we set up a system which is so perfect that we help maximum number of people and also keep helping them year after year?"

He had the correct tone. He looked around to see the look of anticipation on people's faces.

"We kept going to the village and kept talking to them. What we realized was that there were two types of people: one, who were self-employed and the other who were working for others. Obviously, the ones who were employed by the others were terribly poor. We realized that these people actually needed very little amount of money to get started."

The crowd showed signs of agreement. Many of them must have noticed the same from spending years in Toranagallu.

"But they can never muster this money on their own and often spend their lives in labour. Obviously, the bank doesn't help the poor because they may not return the money, apart from other hassles involved.

A farmer cannot assure a bank that he will be able to return a ten thousand rupee loan. A small shop owner cannot convince ICICI or SBI that his shop will do the required business.

This is where the Social Service Department came in. We started disbursing very small loans of about ten thousand rupees to these people with no questions asked. We started a drive to lend small loans to everybody who knocked at Lala Steel's door. All they had to do was to fill a small form and they would be eligible for a loan of up to ten thousand rupees. We started informing the village locals of this scheme and the villagers welcomed us with open arms.

The amount we decided was ten thousand rupees. With a budget of ten crores, we could touch enough people to have transformed this region of Karnataka.

Moreover, this money is not lost. Many of these men have started returning the money as well. We have followed up on a hundred of these people and their business plans have been running on track. We are optimistic about their returning rates."

Shubhro had stuck to the layman language while explaining his project so that people from every branch or department could understand. Everyone in the hall had a reason to be up on his or her feet. Shubhro's speech was welcomed by a loud applause. Everybody in the auditorium loved his vision. Only Shubhro could have thought of such an idea. He had entered the Department and revolutionized it in a matter of two and a half months.

I was amazed by his speech. I looked at Shubhro and wondered who he *really* was. When you see his resume, you would expect a business suit clad sophisticated man to walk in. But he would come in smelling of weed and drains. In the first glance, he would look like a hippie who did not care about a thing in the world. When you talked to him for a brief while, most people would say he is a nut case. Then, you might say that he is nymphomaniac, a *tharki,* who should be kept at least a few yards away.

But here I was. Just a month back, a deprived kid had treated him like God. And today, I was suddenly told that he had changed lives of almost a whole district in Karnataka. This guy was truly unfathomable.

Shubhro was the hero of that gathering. At Lala Steel, departments had announced record outputs. Some departments fought with others for supremacy. But I hadn't seen any reaction close to this one. Everybody loved what the Social Service Department were doing. Shubhro was the man of the hour.

I thought of the day when Shubhro had mentioned that he wanted to work for Lala Steel. He had said he thought this was the least meaningless job that he could think of. At that time, I had dismissed the thought as just another idea from an evening full of weed. But now, I realized that he had thought of it from to the core of his heart. He had truly believed in the concept.

The final applause was followed by a question and answer round.

"Where did you work before this? Who are you really? How did you reach here?" were the first few questions that were asked.

The answer was going to be interesting. Shubhro had had a colourful past. The true answer would have scandalized a few people, especially the weed part.

"I would appreciate no personal questions please," Shubhro said with a serious expression. The happy mood in the hall dropped for a short moment.

I was not the only one who had thought that his deep black eyes were intriguing. I now knew there were even more stories under that black hair than I knew.

There were more questions asked to Shubhro about how he reached the grass root in spite of the language barrier which Shubhro answered with a smile.

By the end of the session, every girl in the hall had a crush on Shubhro and every man in the hall swore to his life that he had known Shubhro was a genius all along. The Social Service Department was going to be the star of that quarter.

I met Shubhro in the evening, over dinner. He had wanted to go out and I was looking forward to meeting him. There was a lot I wanted to discuss. A lot of questions I wanted to ask. Even though I knew it won't be easy to make him respond.

And it wasn't. I realized it was impossible to make Shubhro talk about what he didn't want to. I was soaked in the thoughts of his mystery. I was trying to read every expression that crossed his face. I was trying very hard to *crack* the code of the guy.

But there was no hope. It was just a pleasant dinner, where I got no closer to knowing him better.

Chapter 23
The Ninetieth Day with Shubhro

I got up in the morning and looked at the calendar. I stroked off the day's date and wrote 'The ninetieth day with Shubhro' over it. Tomorrow this time, I would know whether Shubhro was going to stay or not. Tomorrow would be my last day at Lala Steel. I had my usual corn flakes with milk for breakfast.

It was weird that Shubhro and I had never discussed his departure. Had I asked him the question, it was possible that he would give a straight answer and end the suspense. It was also possible that his reaction might make the answer too obvious.

But right now, I was hoping that the love in his eyes was not an illusion. It was for real.

As I opened my door in the morning to leave, I saw Shubhro standing there.

"Can I keep your keys for the day?" he asked.

"What? Why?" I was bemused. He had never asked for such a thing.

"Just have some faith and let me have your keys. Trust me you would not regret it," he said with a confident smile.

Shubhro had developed multiple number of smiles, depending upon the situation. Some people master the sheepish smile, some master the wicked smile while some people master the mocking smile. But Shubhro had mastered each and every type of smile. Each was as convincing as the other.

I had to give him the keys. How do you argue with a smile like that?

He was my personal Hugh Grant. He was a perfect look alike of Hugh even though he was a Bengali with black eyes. He had made life liveable in this city. As I worked in the office, tea breaks kept taking my thoughts back to him. What exactly was he doing in my room? There was definitely a surprise planned for me.

'Trust me you would not regret it,' Shubhro had said.

It was the second last day of my notice period at Lala Steel. Amit was the only real friend I had left here after Malappa had been roasted. Even though we had started spending less time together after Shubhro had barged into my life, Amit and I had still managed to become great friends. I had never thought I was going to miss somebody who put a bucket of mustard oil in his hair every day. But as I had expected while leaving Delhi, his chivalry and sweetness had been huge assets in this place.

Amit met me over lunch.

"Do you even have a job in hand, Saumya?" Amit asked.

"No, Amit. I will go to Delhi and then see what I can do. I know I should be working on my resume every night. It's no easy task to inflate every project as if it was ten times more challenging. But then, Shubhro is way too interesting. Moreover, today is his ninetieth day," I said.

"Are you..." Amit said but stopped.

"What, Amit? Say it," I said, encouraging him.

"Are you in love with him?"

Finally the question was out in the open, the question which had hung in the air for months and months.

Was I in love with him?

He set my heart racing every time I looked at him. He occupied my mind more than all other things combined. All the symptoms were there. I loved him like a nineteen year old.

And it wasn't hidden from Amit as well. All his remaining doubts must have gotten wiped out with my reaction to the question. There was no going back now.

"So you *are* in love with him," Amit said. I stayed silent. I didn't know the response.

"So what are you going to do? He will leave tomorrow morning!" Amit said as he put another spoon of the terrible *dal* and rice in his mouth.

"It is a simple equation, Amit. Tonight might be his ninetieth night in Toranagallu, but he had once stayed back in Rio de Janeiro because he fell in love with the place and its people. So if his love for me is as intense as mine is for him, then I am sure he would stay back. But if it is only me then he would leave," I said.

"Hmm. I understand. But what are you going to do?"

"If tomorrow morning Shubhro is not here, I would stick to my resignation. I would pack my bags and move on. But if Shubhro would have stayed, then I might stay back. I am sure he would have thought of some plan for the two of us. I would leave it on him."

Amit was a little taken aback. "So you are leaving the decision of your career to an Indian Hippie."

"Yes, I am. I love that Hippie."

This was the first time I had actually said it. The assumption that Amit knows it had made it way too easy. The words just popped out of my mouth as if I had forgotten that this is something not supposed to be said. But it was true.

Whoever I met in the corridor that day gave me a reason to not leave Lala Steel. I smiled and dodged every reason.

Shubhro kept coming back to my mind all day. Today would be the last time that I would leave the office feeling good about meeting Shubhro at home. I would no longer be welcomed by Shubhro with the most de-stressing smile in Toranagallu. No more would I have him handy whenever I would need an advice over any matter at all.

―

I finished the day as early as I could. I was anxious to find out what Shubhro was up to. I had an idea what Shubhro was capable of from the seventeen dinners and nine drinking sessions that I had had with him. I made a list of the possibilities Shubhro could have thought of:

- He could have cooked some dishes I would have never heard of from some cuisine I would have never heard of
- He could have decorated my room with flowers and balloons and written my name on the wall with paper cuttings
- He could have made me some beautiful gift using something from the room
- Or maybe he would have hid my gift somewhere in the room and left a treasure hunt for me to find it

I imagined the triumphant moment when Shubhro's idea would turn out to be one of these. Sitting in the office bus, I wrote down the possibilities on a piece of paper so that I can prove to Shubhro that I had already thought of these possibilities.

I reached the corridor of my room and saw that my room looked completely normal from the outside. I had come earlier than usual. I did not want to enter with him being unprepared. But Shubhro had had my room for nine hours. They were more than enough.

I felt the excitement as I opened my door. I had biggish expectations from Shubhro.

Trust me you will not regret it.

The room was far from decorated. In fact, Shubhro seemed to

have dishevelled it further. The kitchen slab was exactly as I had left it. Shubhro was sleeping on my bed in nothing but his boxers. I hated seeing men who used boxers and shorts interchangeably. People need to know boxers are underwear.

I woke him up by slapping his back. Okay, not his back but his cute ass. I was feeling irritated and cheated, having discovered nothing till now.

"Shubhro, why did you take my room key?"

Shubhro was still half asleep. He had a habit of keeping his face in the pillow instead of the back of his head.

I repeated "Shubhro, why did you take my room key?"

It took me good fifteen minutes to get him to hear me. He was deep asleep. Finally I got him to sit up and listen to what I was saying. He had to answer now.

"Hey, Saumya. How was your day?" He got up and slipped into his cotton pyjamas.

"Shut up and answer my question."

"Oh that. Well Saumya, the air conditioner in my room in my guest house was not working."

I felt like slapping him on his face and I did. But there was a difference in the slap I wanted to give and the one I did give. I had wanted to give a brutal, insulting slap. But the slap I gave was a friendly affectionate slap. I didn't have it in me to deliver a hard slap.

Trust me you will not regret it.

"And you left me to wonder as to what you were planning for me." I let the emotion flow.

"I know. Actually the air conditioner in my room is perfectly fine. I just wanted you to think of me the whole day." And he flashed a romantic smile. All conversations are normal until he brings out a smile from his bag. After all it was all but a one sided affair. I had been defeated but I was not going to accept it.

"That's not done Shubhro. I want you out of the room now. I don't want to see your face. You spoiled my whole day. And yes, both of us are having dinner alone today in our respective rooms."

Shubhro played surprisingly obedient. It seemed he had expected me to be touched by his corny line.

I just wanted you to think of me all day.

I was not nineteen years old. Or maybe I was.

Shubhro left and I decided to change to my pyjamas and relax. I opened my cupboard.

My cupboard had a huge packet which was a gift packed in flashy red. The first thing I did was to rush to the door and check if Shubhro had left. He was standing at my doorstep as if he had just rung the bell.

He had expected me to open the cupboard within a few minutes of his departure. His romantic smile got broader and more piercing. I called him in and returned to the gift. The fact that the box was huge-ish escalated my excitement to bigger highs.

I opened the wrapping paper. The box had a bottle of French

Rose Wine and a pair of wine glasses. The bottle looked beautiful.

Shubhro looked at me and said "Authentic Bordeaux Rose Wine. I had gone to see a friend, all the way to Hampi yesterday while you were at office. I had asked him to bring this wine for you. I am sure you would like it."

We cooked that evening. We had to restrain ourselves from starting with wine but we wanted to have wine like the French. We wanted to have it with dinner.

I managed a *dal* with rice. There was no table or chair in my room. One had to eat sitting on the bed. The Rose wine looked beautiful in the wine glasses. The two glasses with pink coloured wine, kept with the bottle was photographable stuff.

For Shubhro, it was a day of wine stories. I wondered how many stories had he told me in the ninety days we had spent together. Even if he had been telling me ten a day, it would mean nine hundred stories. I wondered how many times he had told each one of them. And how many had he accumulated in this trip.

How would he tell the story where he swept me off my feet with his gift?

I wondered how many girls had felt weak in their knees on hearing those stories. I definitely felt very weak.

We drank late into the night. Shubhro's wine drunkenness was different from Shubhro's beer drunkenness. Beer got him blabbering. Wine got him talking. Being deprived of weed for so long, wine must have given him some respite.

I was expecting Shubhro to make a move sooner or later. He did at around one o'clock. He moved his head forward to kiss me. I moved my head backwards and successfully avoided his lips.

Kissing him would have led to other things. The thought of the morning on the ninety first day had scared me plenty of times. And now it was only a few hours away. The clock had started clicking before I would have no clue where he was.

I felt as if I would have to pay back for every bit of fun that I was having right now. I would have to shed a tear corresponding to every smile that I have now. The more I would get involved, the more pain I will experience.

The wine had a maddening effect on Shubhro in some ways. He had the look in his eyes. For a second I thought he would bring out his just-kissing smile after that look but it hung on. He was serious. He was up to something.

Shubhro took a step back. He maintained a plain face and I kept wondering what he was up to. He bent one of his knees and looked straight into my eyes. I realized it was the proposal posture. He had gotten down proposing to me. Ecstatic.

"Saumya, I wanted to write down something for you but I knew that I could not have predicted how I would be feeling at this moment. What I say right now should be exactly how I am feeling at this very moment as we stand here. It would not have been fair if I had written something for you before and said it now. There is a lot that I have to say and please, *please* let me say it."

I had fallen in love with the different types of smile that Shubhro could bring out of his bag. I had believed his smile was what worked for him. But today, I got to know that he had another expression which could rock my insides like nothing ever had. It was his look of intensity with all the seriousness in Karnataka.

"They say that you can never be friends with somebody you once loved. If you can be, then you were never in love. My case is a little different. We have been friends and now I am in love with you. But I cannot be friends with you anymore. I love you, Saumya. There cannot be friendship between us."

He gulped some more wine.

"You are beautiful Saumya and I mean physical beauty here. But the only catch is, that if I were to sit down and make a list of great things about you, that point would probably be way down the list. There are a million things about you that make my head swirl. You are just perfect. I love you Saumya, I really do."

He actually used the L word. I was expecting he would tell me how much he liked me but I did not expect him to actually tell me that he *Loved* me. My heart, stomach, liver, kidney everything melted at that moment.

Meanwhile, he continued.

"I have known you for three months and in these three

months, my affection for you has gone only up and up and up and now it has reached a level that there is no going back. I want you to be mine. I love you Saumya, I really do."

There was no scope of doubt in every word that he pronounced. There was force of conviction in his voice. There was no way anybody would have ever had that much certainty in his voice.

"There came a point when realization dawned on me and I saw that I am in love with you. My initial reaction was to try and fall out of love with you. Soon, I realized that it was impossible and that I should stop these futile attempts and accept that I, after all, am human and fully capable of falling in love. I know we come from completely different worlds Saumya. I know there are things about you that I will never be able to understand and there are things about me that you will never understand but still, I love you Saumya, I really do."

He held the back of my neck with firm fingers. There was no hint of any sort of goofing around in his body movement. He meant what he was doing. Still holding my neck, he started pushing my head forward as he brought his own head forward. I later realized that he did give me a chance to back out. I could have thrown my head back. Shubhro hadn't really forced me. He only wanted me to believe that I did not have an option except succumbing.

Our lips touched. Initially for a few seconds, it was only him kissing me. My head was too busy analysing the pros and the cons of kissing him. I kept thinking of the moment when

I would find out that he had left and shuddered at the thought.

And then slowly, I let all the doubts melt away and I fervently kissed him back.

I had imagined this feeling numerous times. I had thought that the touch of his silken lips on mine would erase all my doubts and it did. It was heavenly and Shubhro worked like an artist. He touched me all over and I let him. He had a right to every part of my body.

"Hey, there is one more talent of mine that you are not aware of," Shubhro said, bringing me back to reality.

"Is it? What is it? Which family, in which city, in which country had taught you that?" I teased him.

"I was born with this one. It's the kind of thing I do when I am either touched or overwhelmed," he said as I got up to a semi reclined position, unable to understand which talent he was now referring to.

"I just love writing poetry and some lines are coming to my mind for you," He said as he tweaked my nose playfully.

Having seen Shubhro the way I had, I used to completely forget that Shubhro is also well educated. If he would walk into a bank with a well-made resume, he could easily get a salary package better than mine.

He made some funny sounds which could have meant something in French but were way beyond my comprehension.

The poem was in French. From Shubhro's mouth, it sounded like music. I had not gotten even a single word of what he had said but I was flattered already, even before he had translated.

"It doesn't really translate well. But this is how it would look in English:

You are my new parameter,
My new definition of romance.
The light of my night,
The fire in my belly.
Let's burn the candles,
Let's write the poetry.
Let the pigs fly.
Let it be said,
That this is love."

This was the end of the last bit of inhibitions I had that night.

His experience was evident in his every movement. There was a surety in the way his hands caressed my body. He spent adequate time at every stage of the whole process that night. His movements were gradual and measured.

When he kissed me, he kissed me to my heart's content .

When he took my shirt off, he made me feel complete. I shuddered and shivered with pleasure as his fingers traced lines on my back and moaned as he reminded me of my womanhood.

I quivered with desire as a delightful fire lit my body when he claimed me. He was the God of love, even looked the part and he showed me that it was natural for him to make me go mad.

I had let the inhibitions drop. I loved him. I lusted for him.

Shubhro was an acupuncturist in bed. He knew each and every soft point of the body. He touched me where it tickled the most.

His dusky skin shone in the dark. His pointed nose looked beautiful. He was a visual delicacy.

When we lay spent next to each other, I turned to him and whispered in his ear," The moments we spent together Shubhro make all the suffering worth it. It redeems the tough month. I really, really love you, Shubhro."

I decided I would stay up all night and held him like my teddy bear. I did not have the strength to discover that he was gone in the morning.

And where could he even go from Toranagallu? The receptionist at the guest house would not let him leave without settling a huge bill. I did not expect him to have the money.

I argued with myself and finally concluded that even if he would decide to leave his luggage behind and just leave, he would not have the money to buy the train ticket. Even if he could muster the money, he would have to wait till the late afternoon for the first train. I could easily catch him at the Railway Station.

It was no mean task to run away from Toranagallu. There was a huge exit barrier to the place.

I wondered if it will be a good idea to just ask him his plan. If he planned on leaving, at least I could kiss him good bye. He did not have to leave unnoticed. But what if he had forgotten that it was his ninety first morning tomorrow. Had my love really been so strong? I had seen the I-am-in-love smile on his face. There was no way he had faked it. I would have known.

Even if he was going to leave, couldn't he take me along when he left? There was no way I would make his travels any less fun. Couldn't I just confront him and ask him to take me along? I would promise to comply with his move-on-theory for the rest of my life. I would quit everything for him.

Or would I want to quit everything when I wouldn't have the wine in my blood?

I cursed Shubhro and his bull shit theory. It might have led him to a lot of things but it definitely did not work for me. May his theory be burnt in hell and roasted alongside chicken legs.

I remember seeing six o'clock on the clock. Shubhro was holding me from the back. Our bodies were touching from the head till the toes. He cuddled me as if protecting me from the world's evil. I was love struck.

Chapter 24
The Ninety First Morning

When I checked the time to be ten in the morning, it did not strike me that Shubhro was supposed to be lying next to me. Once it did strike me, my initial reaction was panic.

I considered the possibilities.
- He could have gone back to his room to sleep more comfortably
- He could have gone to the market to fetch milk
- He could have left for good on the ninety first morning

The last possibility was scary. If he had actually left, my world would come tumbling down.

I got dressed quickly and left for the market. The milkman had not seen him all morning.

Strike 1. My heart palpated a little bit.

I then went to the guest house and checked his room. It was locked.

Strike 2. My heart sank.

I went to the reception and asked where the man in room C 206 was.

"He left this morning ma'am. He settled all the bills."

Strike 3. My heart stopped beating that moment.

This was happening for real then. All my hopes of having changed Shubhro had proven to be false. For all I knew, leaving Toranagallu might have been easier than any other place for him. May be he was even counting the days so that he could run away. Maybe he loved weed much more than he ever loved me. But it was a little hard to believe.

"Has he left any messages?" I asked the receptionist, getting desperate.

"No, ma'am but he tipped the staff quite heavily."

He hadn't even left any messages about where he was going. My only hope now was to catch him at the Railway Station.

I asked the receptionist "did you book him a cab till the Railway Station?"

"No, ma'am. We booked him a cab till Hospet."

This was dead end. There was no way to find out a man who had left three hours ago for Hospet in a cab. He was now lost forever. I had had the last piece of information on Shubhro's whereabouts and it wasn't very precise either. I hated having met Shubhro at all.

Curses to his Move-on-Theory. By now he would have bought weed somewhere on his way to Hospet and would be smoking up in the backseat of the cab.

I came back to my room and searched all over if he had left any note or message for me. Or may be some hint about where he was going next. But he hadn't. He had just left in accordance with what he had been doing for three years.

Tired, I sat down on the floor as I gave up the search. A few tears rolled down my cheek and fell on the floor.

All my biggest fears had proven true this morning. Shubhro had left and left me devastated. I was suffering as much as I had feared. I was paying back for every smile. I was suffering for every second that our lips had touched. My body had many proofs of the previous night. His teeth had left marks close to my collarbones. My insides felt as if something had been there very recently. My body felt different from the night that we had had.

Because of the eventful morning, I completely forgot that this was the last day of my notice period. People would have been expecting to say bye to me. Mr Ashish would be looking forward to a final exit interview.

The Exit interview was scheduled at three in the afternoon. I reached only just in time and went straight to Mr Ashish's office.

"Hello, Saumya. It is great to see you today. You look a little off the beat? All is well?"

"Yes, sir. Just a little sleep deprived. I was with friends till late night yesterday."

"Hmm... okay. So as a part of the procedure, I need to ask you whether you still want to leave the company. If yes, why?"

"Sir, this question has played on my mind for three months now and all throughout these three months, I was pretty sure that I want to quit. Especially if the circumstances would be what they are right now."

I meant if Shubhro would have left at the three month mark. I did not want to explain to him the full situation.

"But sir, as I sit here today, I ask myself that what I want to do next. Everything seems so meaningless. What am I running after? What do I even want to do? But I know, having come this far in life, it will be impossible to not do anything at all. It will drive me to insanity. I have to do something to turn the days into the nights.

So I sat down and wondered what would be the least meaningless thing to do at this stage. I don't intend on being a quitter sir. I won't be able to look at my dad in the eye if I did. But I definitely want to quit this job profile. I just don't see a point in it anymore."

I could hear Shubhro speaking through myself. I remember him having said the exact same things as I was saying at this stage.

I continued "but then, I cannot deny that I have learnt more about life in these three months than I must have done in the rest of my life. I have matured and understood the world in a better way. I just wish to go back home to Delhi for two weeks and recharge my batteries. Some big events have happened in my life very recently. I just need to refocus. And then I can adopt my job profile."

"And what kind of profile would you want to work on?"

"I am very clear in that regard. There is only one profile that I am going to work on and that is with Laxmi ma'am. That is definitely the least meaningless job that I can think of. I wish to give away small loans and see the smile on the people's faces when their unimaginable dreams come true. I have known

Mr Shubhro at a personal level and have been deeply influenced by his beliefs. I wish to propagate his agenda further. I wish to continue what he had set rolling."

Mr Ashish was definitely taken aback. He must have expected me to walk in and either resign straight away or just demand an exorbitant amount of salary. That was the decorum in exit interviews.

"Are you dissatisfied with your salary? Do you demand an increment?" Mr Ashish preferred to ask straight away. For a moment I thought if he wanted me to demand an increment. If more money meant I would stay here longer, it was going to be worth it for him.

"No, sir. I am happy with my salary," I said with a smile. I wasn't staying here for money. Moreover, you could never spend a significant amount in Toranagallu.

"You know, Saumya, I had rated you highly from the beginning. But I always thought that you will do great sitting in front of a laptop and getting a job done. But it was on that day when there was a mob on our gate that I realized your true potential. On that day I realized that in a bunch of management trainees, you would definitely stand out because of your sharpness. You have won me over by your choice today. I can tell you that it has been a pleasure working with you."

With this he shook my hand and the meeting ended on a happy note.

The thoughts had been there in my head all day but now I heard them in my voice. Listening to the thoughts put across in such well-structured manner made my head a lot cleaner about them. I had had my share of uncertainty about going back. Suddenly I felt great about going back to Delhi.

My two week leave was approved in no time. That was the only major result of the exit interview. I could not wait to hit Delhi.

As I packed my bags in the evening, I came across a bag of Debenhams. It reminded me of the bet I had had with Vartika. The bet was whether I would be able to use this Debenham lingerie in Toranagallu with my boyfriend.

Strictly speaking I had lost the bet. On that night with Shubhro, I was too clouded with love to have thought of these. I was too unprepared to have used them.

But in reality, the bet was more about finding a man to love in this place. I might not have managed to open the bags but I had definitely found love of an intensity I would have never found, even in Delhi.

Therefore, I could easily convince myself that I had won the bet.

I left behind everything that could possibly remind me of work. I left behind my Toranagallu sim card and switched to the Delhi sim card in my mobile phone. My laptop had not been turned off from the day it had been bought. I left it in Toranagallu without turning it off. I took no books either.

PART 4: After the After Effects

Chapter 25
Being Subdued Is Due

I came back to Delhi and everybody had only one thing to say.

"How come you have subdued so much?"

"Why are you not as bubbly as before?"

"You have matured so much in four months."

I had no clue how to react to this. I did not even know whether to take this as a compliment or be sad about it. When I saw my room, I saw the pink paint on the wall and the Hugh Grant poster on my wall. For a moment, I honestly thought it was Shubhro's picture. I saw his picture in my phone to compare it with him and marvelled at the similarity.

I took off the poster from the wall so that it doesn't remind me of him. But the empty space that the poster left behind reminded me of not trying to remember him. The purpose got defeated anyway.

I opened my cupboard and the skirts and shorts didn't interest me anymore. I had no interest left in being the centre of any conversation. I did not want to be noticed or known. I just wanted to meet Mommy and Vartika.

I was meeting Vartika and Sunny in a nearby restaurant. I had reached early and been waiting.

Vartika walked into the restaurant and gave her version of compliments.

"I like your new style statement. It is much more mature. When I see you now, I feel… earlier you were so flashy and wanna-be."

"And how is it now?" I asked.

"It's much more natural now. It seems you are not going out of your way to look good."

It seemed absolutely genuine from the way she said it. In spite of everything that had changed, it was still heartening to see that hint of jealousy and admiration when she said it. She said I could have traded a thousand compliments for this one. Vartika became such a darling all over again.

Ten minutes later, Sunny walked in as well. He was tall and Delhi's summer had tanned him a hint more from the last time. He was handsome in an unconventional way. He must be a good boyfriend to have.

"So what was Toranagallu like?" asked Sunny.

There was no mocking in his voice. We had grown over that stage. It was no fun to pull my leg over this topic. Or maybe I looked just way too subdued to be jeered at.

"It was great. Totally." It really was. I had gained more experiences in a few months in Toranagallu than people do in a life time.

"Hmm," Vartika intervened. "So did you win the bet? Were you able to use those pair of Debenhams that I had given you at the Railway Station? I so wish you did with that Bengali guy of yours. What was his name... yeah, Shubhro."

The mention of Shubhro's name from Vartika's mouth was disturbing. She was expecting him to be a happy memory. I did not even know if he was a happy or a sad memory. It would take some time for me to find out.

I told Vartika and Sunny everything: About how I met Shubhro and his beliefs. What I had thought he was and what he actually was.

There was silence once I was done telling them.

I was waiting in anticipation. Sunny and Vartika were silent because they knew I was waiting in anticipation.

"So? What do you guys think?"

"What is there to think? You messed up big time Saumya!" Vartika said. "How can you even have second thoughts about running away with him? He was such a wonderful guy, honey. And he loved you! And you loved him. What else did you want?"

I was looking at her in silence. She was saying exactly what I had feared to hear from her.

"Why didn't you just tell him that you were dying to run away with him? Why did you wait till he was gone forever?" Vartika could feel my pain.

I looked at her and wanted to dig a hole in the restaurant floor and bury myself.

I looked at Sunny and I could see that he was deliberately

trying to avoid my eye.

"What Sunny? What do you think?" I asked him.

"You don't want to know, girls."

"We do," we said in a chorus.

"Well," Sunny said. "What are you telling me Saumya…? That you really believe he loved you? The only reason that he proposed to you was because you would not let him enter your pants unless he told you so. He waited till the last day because that's when you would be at your vulnerable best. It all fits in, Saumya. I respect the guy for his heart of gold but I can't deny that he was a total pervert. He is what I had always wanted to be."

Sunny had the guy's perspective to the situation. My thoughts went back to the ninetieth day with Shubhro, when he had gone down on one knee, and opened his heart out. How could he possibly have been faking it? Can it all be pretence?

But Sunny had been around the world which added credibility to his opinion. There was no reason why I should have absolutely discarded his opinion as absolute junk.

And yet, I did, acting like a nineteen year old.

I spent the first week treating myself with stuff I had missed in Toranagallu. I had samosas and *gol gappe*. I bought a stack of books and read all through the night. I bought a new phone, now that I could afford any. I bought a HiDesign bag and felt jubilant for thirty seconds.

And then I was back to my normal self.

I kept trying my best to not think of Shubhro.

But whenever I would see a Bengali on the road, my thoughts would travel back to him.

Whenever I would see someone play the guitar, my thoughts would travel back to him.

Whenever I would see a kissing scene in a movie, my thoughts would travel back to him.

In fact, whenever I saw any form of romance, my thoughts would travel back to him.

Whenever I saw the colour of his favourite shirt, my thoughts would travel back to him.

Whenever I would smell any fragrance my thoughts would go back to him.

I tried to shop to lift my spirits but it was only marginally useful.

The two weeks went past in a jiffy. There were enough friends to catch up, enough eateries to visit, enough relatives to touch feet of and enough books to read.

This time around, when I took the train to Toranagallu, I was surer of myself. And that was obviously because I clearly knew what I was getting myself into this time. I was going this time by choice rather than by chance. The part of me which was looking forward to it was contesting with the part of me which was still scared.

It was time I got life back into perspective.

As I thought of Shubhro, I regretted having not offered him to take me with him. Why had I not even touched the topic for ninety days with him? Why had I been so optimistic that he won't leave? And that bastard, couldn't he ask me to come along when he was leaving. Why couldn't he move on with me? Would I make his journey any less fun?

The whole train journey I kept thinking of him and wondering if he would be thinking of me as well. I also wondered if he would have gotten back to his hippie ways in some part of the world. I didn't even know if he was still in India or not. He could have been in Philippines for all I knew.

I reached my room and kept my bags. It had been a while since I had sat with my laptop. I felt a Facebook craving. I had had so many better things to do that I hadn't logged into Facebook for a long time. Not since I had sat in my office and wondered what surprise Shubhro would be throwing for me. It seemed like a different era now: A golden era which I would like to freeze and not tamper with for anything in the world.

Chapter 26
His Story

I took out my laptop which was still turned on. It was in Stand By mode for conserving battery.

I lifted its screen and pressed enter to bring it back to life. I saw that Microsoft Internet Explorer had been left on. The page that was open was a blog. The blog was called Wandering Viewfinder. I had never seen the page before. I had definitely not left it opened. Somebody else had used the laptop and opened that page.

I scrolled down to check the popularity of the blog. The first post had three hundred and fifty four comments. That meant it must be a very popular blog on the internet.

My eyes read some keywords like 'Trinidad and Tobago, Brazil, Photography, Toranagallu.'

There was only one intersection possible of these keywords in this world. The author had to be Shubhro.

Everything became obvious to me. That ninetieth night when I had gone off to sleep, Shubhro had been awake all the time. He had waited for me to have completely slept off. When he got the opportunity, he opened this link on my laptop and left without a word. It was as if he wanted to say something through his blog.

I clicked on 'About the Author' link of the blog. Shubhro had not uploaded his own picture. His name Shubhro was mentioned nowhere. The only name he used for himself was 'Wandering Viewfinder'. He had left no possibility of being traced. Only people who had met him knew who he was.

Shubhro had left the link opened on my laptop before leaving. I decided to visit the earliest ever post on the blog.

It read 'My story'. It had to be the childhood story of Shubhro. I thought of the day when I had met Shubhro in Hampi. He had mentioned a little stuff about his days in his MBA but nothing before that. I could not wait to read about his childhood days on the blog.

Here is the article:

"Hi. I am Wandering Viewfinder. I am not the guy you would want to take to your parents and introduce as your friend. I do a lot of things which I shouldn't and wouldn't tell my kids. But I still do them.

I was born in Kolkata India in 1984. As I write this, I am 23 years old. My mother had a coffee shop in Kolkata. She was as Bengali as any woman can be. Every morning, she would take out a neatly ironed and starched *sari* and wear in a way which would ooze class and elegance. My father was born and brought up in Asansol, which is a town near Kolkata. My father hid himself in a goods train coming from Asansol to Kolkata and had reached some part of Kolkata. He was homeless, penniless in the city. He would work in the yard in the day and drink away the money in the night.

But after some time, he needed some stability. This was when he met my mother and made her fall in love with himself. Soon, they got married and my father got a home for the first time in Kolkata.

My mother took my father also into the coffee shop and together they made decent money. I was born in the third year of their marriage. My father would work in the coffee shop in the day and drink away whatever money he could get his hands on.

Things between him and my mother started going astray from the tenth year of their marriage. There had been fights before but the tenth year onwards, things began to go haywire.

Or maybe things had always been haywire but I began to see only when I had reached a stable age.

I started hating my father quite early in life. I was eleven years old when my mother asked my father for divorce for the first time. He beat her up when she said this. The second time she asked him for divorce was when I was fifteen years old. He beat both of us, her and me, this time. Ten minutes into beating me he then asked me to drink his glass of whisky. To date, I have not been able to understand the pleasure he had derived by making me drink his whisky that night. But he would make me take a sip and would slap me if I hesitated. It took me three minutes to finish my first ever glass of whisky.

Once the stigma was dropped, one thing led to another and by the time I was nineteen, I needed weed every weekend.

Coke was occasional but beer had become my water.

All throughout my childhood, all I saw was bickering and shouting between the two of them. And then one fine day, when I was twenty, I decided to literally throw my father out of the home. My friend Tamal was there with me. I am not exaggerating. We threw him out of the house, in a way that he could not have fought his way back. His chapter was closed that day. My mother was just watched with a stolid expression.

Life improved instantaneously. The next month, my mother convinced me into entering rehab for drugs. I told her I am not addicted but both of us knew that it was a lie. Both of us knew, I could not have said no to her because I loved her.

I succumbed and went to the rehab. Fortunately, the rehab proved completely successful. Our home was wiped of one evil after the other. Once my fucking father left, my drugs followed their way out. And then, my studies also picked up. At the age of twenty one, I entered IIM Kolkata, one of the best B schools in India.

My stay at the B school was a roller coaster ride. I had the time of my life but stayed away from any kinds of drugs. The corridors would have a smell of weed all through the day but I restrained from any sort of indulgence. I had only one girlfriend in my whole stay. I was a good boy.

My summer internship was at Standard Chartered Bank in Mumbai. That was where I met Mr Anderson. Mr Anderson played saxophone at a club in Trinidad and Tobago. I had met Mr Anderson in the summer of 2004. We had discussed the possibilities of small loans in Trinidad and Tobago at that time itself and the way we can improve the lives of so many people. I loved the concept of affecting so many lives. Sitting over a beer, we had chalked out a detailed plan for the whole project. However, once the plan was on paper, both of us knew that I did not have the time to go ahead and implement it. As much as I would have loved to help him, I was engrossed in finishing my MBA. Once I would be done with my MBA, I would get busy with my job. There was no way I could have managed the time to quit everything and execute it.

My mother had been running her coffee shop for twenty seven years now. Our expenditures had grown in leaps and bounds but her income had been quite stagnant. As a result, we were hardly making ends meet by the time I graduated. We were hard pressed for money. My mother had been working extremely hard in order to save the money on the salary she would have to pay a helping hand. She lived a tough life.

So the day my placement interviews started, I was particularly kicked about getting a good job and tell my mom to start resting. For twenty seven years, she had hardly taken a vacation. I wanted her to take a break and travel to USA.

Standard Chartered Bank was the first interview I gave and nobody was surprised when I was told in the interview itself that I am selected. I kissed my girlfriend and headed home to tell my mother that I had got a job.

When I reached home, my mother did not open the door. She had had a heart attack and died a silent death in her bed. She never lived to know that I had got a job.

I could never savour the idea of doing that job anymore.

Everything seemed absolutely meaningless. What is the point of earning money? What is the point in even being rich?

At this point I thought of the least meaningless job to do. And the only answer I got was to work with Mr Anderson in Trinidad and Tobago. My beliefs and theories have changed. I am taking a flight to Trinidad and Tobago tomorrow evening with some clothes and my camera to meet Mr Anderson.

At this point, I had nothing on my mind except to find money and organize it into small loans for poor people in Trinidad and Tobago.

I have no clue where the money will come from and how many people will I help.

I will keep you updated."

This was the earliest ever post of the blog.

The only thought going through my mind was that whether I know this guy at all? I had until now thought that it was the extreme boredom in Toranagallu which had landed Shubhro into giving away small loans for Lala Steel. Suddenly, I got to know that small loans were a lifelong mission that Shubhro had taken up. It was not a hobby. It was a life's mission. Even after that guy had left, he had continued to keep me baffled and confused as to who the real Shubhro was? How can weed and such compassion for fellow people go together? Just when I was beginning to restart my life leaving him behind, he had made a comeback and brought everything crashing down.

Chapter 27
Getting the Money Together

The following posts retold all the stories that I had heard from Shubhro every evening for those three months. It was déjà vu of the highest order.

Two months after he had left home and reached Trinidad and Tobago, one of his blog posts caught my attention.

"I had left home with ten thousand rupees in my pocket. The most basic resource to support small loans is money. I deeply believe in my heart that every poor man would return all the little money that I give but I need to have the money in the first place to give them.

To support the same, I hereby start collecting money to sustain these loans. These loans are the objective of my life. I had decided at a point that I will quit the race for money completely but if this is what this mission will take then so shall it be.

The three sources of money for this program would be:
- I am putting up advertisements on this blog. These advertisers will pay me money for their publicity

- All the photographs that I put up here can be bought for twenty dollars each
- I will accept donation

I spend the days talking to the locals. Mr Anderson and I talk to them and try and understand a way of helping their cause. All we want to do is make their lives easier in whichever way we can. But starting out has turned out to be a huge task.

The biggest challenge in the whole affair is managing the paper work. I need to understand what kind of commitment has to be taken from the people before approving the loan. This will enable us to touch maximum number of lives with the cash we have. That is all we want to do.

If the move-on theory and I have to survive, I need a steady source of income. As a result, I would now have to put up advertisements on my blog. If you click on them, I would get money and that would fund my travels. I have been told that this thing is good money. I sure hope so.

Thanks,

Wandering Viewfinder"

That explained a lot of things. That explained how Shubhro could leave without letting me know. This explained how he could pay the guest house rupees five hundred per day for a period of three months. He had steady sources of income from which he supported himself as well. Judging from the number of comments he had, I could see he was quite popular and was definitely earning enough money to fund his travels. His photographs were genuinely good even to my naïve eye.

Chapter 28
Here and There

I read each and every blog post and relived all those moments that I had spent with him listening to his stories. God, I missed him.

"Ninety First Day at Rio de Janeiro

As I write this, it is my ninety first day in Rio de Janeiro and I am still in Rio de Janeiro. My plans of establishing small loans in this city have failed big time. The challenges of language, crime and the government have overpowered my commitment for the first time.

This morning, I had two options. I could either accept defeat at the hands of Rio de Janeiro, remembering it as the first city where I could not establish the small loan system or could accept the defeat of the Move-On-Theory and take three more months in this place and implement the loan system in the next three months.

I chose the latter. I decided to invest three more months into this city and try and give away loans. This is going to be the biggest challenge for me up till now.

Wandering Viewfinder"

I thought of the day when he had told me that he had spent six months in Rio de Janeiro. I had sadly assumed that it was because of some love affair that he had stayed back. But it had been because he had not been able to establish loans for the needy in Rio. The feeling of guilt was natural.

This guy was a saint in the disguise of a maverick. He found comfort in being considered a maverick.

I wanted to know what happened thereafter. Did he manage to finally succeed in Rio de Janeiro?

"One Hundred and Eightieth Day in Rio de Janeiro

As I write this, I have just erased a lot of self-doubts I have had for years. I have successfully implemented small loan in Rio de Janeiro. I have made more than a few enemies. Some of the government officers cum mafia bigwigs would love to hunt me down and shoot me. But it was worth it. You should have seen the smiles on those faces. I love what I am doing.

Wandering Viewfinder"

That added another virtue to the list of saintliness of this man, perseverance. I could read through the lines the tens of arguments and threats he must have made to the mafia. The hours of paper work he must have done. The people he must have fought with. He was a real life hero.

Chapter 29
Me

There was no way I could have stopped reading once I had started. I kept reading each and every post on that blog.

Seven hours later, I was still reading the blog posts by Wandering Viewfinder. I had been wondering if he would have written about me anywhere in the blog. And if he would have written about me, would I be just one other friend or somebody special. The blog should clarify a lot of doubts.

Seven hours later, I finally reached the part where Shubhro had written about his stay in Hampi. I read his post on Hampi. He had written about me.

"It has been six months since I have been back in India. I had believed that when love had been so easy and natural in all these cities, it should be even easier in my own land. But it has been quite the contrary.

When I came back, romance did not really live up to the expectations. I had landed in Delhi expecting to see Aishwarya Rai and Frieda Pinto all around me but it wasn't so. In Goa, I had met the kind of beauties I had seen during my travels so that didn't excite me either.

But today, sitting in the middle of Karnataka, at The Mango Tree Restaurant I met this girl called Saumya. She was like a breath of fresh air coming from a steel plant. We drank together and the more I drank, the sexier she got."

"Yippie!" I said to myself. He had liked me from the first day itself. I had liked him even before I had seen his face. The sight of his pyjamas and footwear had been enough to catch my attention.

It seemed that I had always longed for such an approval from Shubhro. From this post, I got to know that he liked the superficial. He liked the way I look and my first impression was a favourable one. It had been mutual from the first day. No matter how mature or grown up a girl gets, such a compliment always means a lot.

Chapter 30
Toranagallu

And then came the big part: The part where he talked about Toranagallu.

He loved me. I was all over his blog. He had never mentioned anyone the way he had talked about me on his blog. It was true, passionate love. He had declared it and talked about it in all the seventeen posts that he had written about Toranagallu. He had mentioned how his belief in The-Move-On theory had never been so weak. He mentioned that he contemplated staying back or at least to ask me if he could start moving on in a pair rather than alone. It had all been mutual. Triumph.

"The Last Day in Hampi

Jean and I were not drinking in celebration.

On the last day, I packed my bag and left with Jean for Sagar Bar like I did every weekend. Jean was waiting with rolling paper and a pack of weed in his hand. Before I got started, I checked a piece of paper my pocket. The paper had Saumya's name and address. I could only get high enough to be able to reach Saumya's place the next morning.

Jean and I started downing one bottle after the other. Weed

intake was quite steady as well. I remember until the point where Jean and I were betting on who can down a bottle of beer faster. Once Jean must have been knocked out for the night, I must have decided to leave for Toranagallu. The only thing I remember is stopping a taxi and getting into it. I must have handed over the paper to him. The taxi driver woke me up at Toranagallu's entrance. The guards must have not let him enter. I must have walked inside.

I found myself in the hospital the next morning. Saumya was sitting beside me in the hospital. The needful had been done. I had reached her, in spite of my own smell. I had achieved yet another successful move on.

Saumya took me to the company guest house. If she had let me stay with her, I could have afforded to give away two more small loans but I could not have told her so. I don't exactly have the image that would let an Indian woman stay with me.

There is rarely a day when I wake up and not pledge to quit weed and beer. And yet there is rarely a day when I touch neither. But today Saumya did something that was quite unprecedented. When she told me to quit, this time I had no energy to fight back the argument. This time, I wanted to comply. The final deal had the following clauses:

- No weed till I am staying here
- Beer only once every week
- Shaving and bathing every week

As she put one condition after the other in front of me, my head was clogged with staring at her smile rather than thinking of a counter argument. I want to live up to my promise this time. For the first time after my mother passed away, I feel like being a good boy once again.

Wandering Viewfinder"

In spite of all the stories Shubhro had told me, there were many many more that he hadn't. It was weird to live through those days from his eyes. His view was very different from mine in some ways. In other ways, his view was surprisingly similar to mine.

Even I had stared at his smile rather than thinking of a counter argument to what he was saying.

Chapter 31
Favour Done By Vartika

"The Fifth Day with Saumya

I had decided that I will wait till the fourth day to start complaining of boredom and ask Saumya to take me to office. It was the fourth day yesterday. So I wrote a suitable mental script to tell her to take me with her. It had the exact same effect as I had thought.

As a result, I was in her office with her today. I met Mrs Laxmi. This whole coup seems to have fitted much better than I had thought. As I type this, I will be working with the exact funds that I had targeted at Lala Steel. With a detailed loan plan, all the money would reach all the people who need it the most.

This is the highest point of my journey of three years. To a distant viewer, The-Move-On-Theory might seem like one long party. From where I stand, it has been constant hardship and pain.

It is fun to say hi to new people. But it is much more difficult to say bye to people who have become very close friends. Men of my age, come close to tears once in many years. I however, cry every three months as I sit in a bus/train/flight to some distant place. I give smiles to strangers but I also give tears to some people who have become really close.

Therefore, I have decided that if things fall in place this time, I shall get easier on myself with the move theory after this. I shall amend the initial constitution and design something which might be more fun. Maybe get a partner in crime. Maybe it will be Saumya. But for the entire world that I have seen, I really don't have the balls to ask her if she would like to come with me.

She is the regular MBA type. You would not expect her to take even one day's leave more than what is allowed to her. Quitting the job and travelling is something that might give her the shudders. And that too with me.

Wandering Viewfinder"

There was also an image attached to the same blog post. The image consisted of my feet.

I now understood why he loved clicking my body parts. He had clicked my feet, my hands, my elbow, my hair. It had all been for this blog. He had taken care that I am not recognizable though. He had ensured that my privacy is not infiltrated. He had taken care.

"The Seventeenth Day with Saumya

Something extremely weird happened today. It was quite unprecedented. As I entered Saumya's room, I saw that she was talking to one of her friend called Vartika on video conferencing.

I sat next to her and saw Vartika on the screen. My first

reaction was that Vartika was quite hot. But I soon realized that I had no inclination towards getting in her pants. This had never happened before. Each time I would see a beautiful girl, I would have to imagine her naked. There was no fault of Vartika. She was even wearing a noodle strap top and shorts. She was much more likeable than many women who have given me countless sleepless nights before. But now, I have lost all desire to kiss any woman except Saumya. I was flirting with Vartika out of habit. The attempts were hollow. I wanted to imagine her naked but it was just not happening. Saumya has monopolized my testosterone to such levels that my hormones have become immune to anybody else's interference.

I had never expected this to happen. No weed, no beer, no lust. I am becoming a girl.

Wandering Viewfinder"

This post made me laugh out loud sitting in my room. Somehow it made me think of how adorable Shubhro actually was. How easily I would give away everything I had to meet him then. I had loved Shubhro but still not expected him to become a loyal cow. Suddenly, I loved him even more than before.

Sitting in my room, I looked around. I hadn't unpacked after coming from Delhi. I had just opened the flap of my laptop and sat on it. I had entered the room with a strong resolve to put Shubhro and his memories behind me. To not to think of him and his memories related to my room every time I would look around.

But stumbling upon his blog did just the reverse. I was

reeking with desire to hug that dusky black eyed boy. I wanted to see that pointed nosed weed addict.

Chapter 32
Who Was He?

"The Forty Seventh Day with Saumya

Today, finally Saumya got the first hint of my work. We bumped into Sridhar, one of the beneficiaries from the small loan of ten thousand rupees. True to his word and as he had promised me, he has started his evening snack shop in Toranagallu. I was initially perturbed about divulging any details. But then I realized that the only reason I was hiding it from her was because I normally don't divulge any details to any one during my travels. It was perfectly ok to tell her. Just that I felt shy about sharing the details. The spoilt Bengali image is so much easier to live up to. Suddenly, I have become everybody's well-wisher who is great at heart. I feel like puking on hearing that description.

Whenever I am asked why am I doing what I am doing, I have never had an answer. The only real answer to this question is that I have to do something in life. Sitting idle at home would be too difficult. And this is what I feel is the least meaningless to be doing. It is relatively easier to fool myself into doing. All I want to do is maximize the number of lives that I am touching and that's all.

Today, at dinner, I saw that the look in Saumya's eyes when she sees me had changed completely. Till now, I had been comfortable in seeing that hint of contempt in her eyes. At least I knew what she was thinking.

But today, there were intimidating questions and curiosity in her eyes. I had every reason to keep shifting posture and be uncomfortable by that look. I love my bad boy rapport, however false it may be.

Wandering Viewfinder"

I remembered that day clearly. That was the first time I had had any clue about the real Shubhro. That was the day my love for Shubhro had undergone a metamorphosis. Until then it had been a school girl love. I had loved his Hugh Grant face. But this was the day that the shallowness in my love had begun to get erased. That was the day I had begun being re-intrigued by Shubhro. And then today I have been intrigued to infinity.

"The Eighty Fourth Day with Saumya

Mrs Laxmi turned out to be a great colleague to work with. Before I joined, she had been single-handedly heading the Social Service Department. I realized on the first day itself that she wasn't the kind of a leader who was equipped to manage such funds.

A natural transition followed and she was more than willing to initiate a smooth exit for herself and give as much responsibility to me as I would have liked. The project began to take shape.

For a month, I kept moving around Toranagallu to meet

the villagers. We differentiated the needy from the pretenders by rigorous interviews and analysis. By the second week, I had truly captured the pulse of the village. We could now start making a list of people who were going to be definite beneficiaries of the small loan of ten thousand rupees.

Things rolled on much smoother than I could have imagined. It was for the first time that I was handling money of this magnitude. Against Mrs Laxmi's ambitious targets, I was also running against my personal time target of three months. Things began to fall in place once I rolled up my sleeves.

By Saturday last week, we had benefited ten thousand people with the small loans. I had never been so satisfied with my own reach.

Wandering Viewfinder"

That was the day when Shubhro transformed from being my hero to everyone's hero. I had been bowled over enough by this part. I was eager to reach the final day he had spent with me. What exactly was he thinking? How tough was it for him?

Chapter 33
The Day

"Final Day with Saumya

I cannot procrastinate the question any more. I have to decide at this point. Whether Saumya will come with me or not. I have no clue whether she wants to come with me or not. All my intuition says that if I ask her directly, she would initially say yes but then develop cold feet. Ideally, if I let her see how life would be without me and then ask her in a few days, my chances would be maximized. But it cannot possibly be done. I have no clue what I am going to do.

I got up early in the morning even though I had finished work a week before. I had intended to ask her to skip office but could not frame it in the right way in my mind. As a result, I ended up not asking her to stay at all. The best I could do was to ask for her key so that at least I can plan the grand evening that I wanted.

I had asked Jean to arrange wine.

It is strange that for the first time, I feel like letting those private moments with Saumya tonight remain private. Each time I looked at her, I wanted to ask her to come along with me. But succumbing into temptation is the devils work. I had no clue whether I was going to ask her to come along or not.

Finally, I thought I would ask.

Wandering Viewfinder"

This was false. Shubhro had left without leaving me a hint of where he was headed.

Lost in these thoughts, I scrolled onto more recent posts. Shubhro was now in Andaman and Nicobar. He had not left without leaving a trace. There was a reason why he had left his blog link opened on my laptop. He had wanted me to know that he was in Andaman and Nicobar. He had wanted me to have an option of finding him out.

Everything he had written on the blog was true.

Shubhro had not left without leaving any hint of where he had Moved-On to...